WHICH
WAY YOU
GONNA JUMP?

WHICH WAY YOU GONNA JUMP?

DONNA VANN

CF4·K

For Lisa, David and Millay -
who always inspire me

Which Way You Gonna Jump?
© Copyright 1998 Donna Vann
Reprinted 2007
ISBN: 978-1-85792-368-1

Published by Christian Focus Publications Ltd,
Geanies House, Fearn, Tain, Ross-shire
IV20 1TW, Scotland, UK.
Tel: 01862 871011
Fax: 01862 871699
www.christianfocus.com
email: info@christianfocus.com

Cover design by Danie van Straaten
Printed and bound in Denmark
Nørhaven Paperback A/S

CONTENTS

Hitler and other minor problems 7

Life on Crazy Street 11

The rock starts to roll 23

Blackie and Whitey 35

My sister, the disaster zone! 45

Trusting is tricky 57

Welcome to the asylum! 69

The park pack 77

My name, my shame 85

Homeless in my home 93

Level One - It begins 105

This Star needs some sparkle 117

Blame it on Chinese takeaways 125

A reason to start hating 137

Out with the Family Secret 147

Get ready for the new Star Smith! 157

A decision I had to make 167

A satisfying splash 183

Not ready to die! 195

Figure it out for yourself 205

Hoping for a return 215

HITLER AND OTHER MINOR PROBLEMS

Our town is as white as a winter postcard snow scene, and I'm not talking about the weather. You'd think it wouldn't be possible in this day and age to find a place so empty of dark faces, but except for a handful of Asians it's just whites everywhere you look. That's why it wasn't surprising Ebony's arrival stirred things up. Changed things, even.

I couldn't help staring at her, the first few weeks of school. Ebony was that kind of person anyway– you'd have stared no matter what colour she was. She sat to the left and slightly in front of me in history, her bushy hair splaying out over the desk of the person behind her. She was tall and thin, but not quite as dark as her name suggested. She seemed to be making tiny movements all the time. You had the feeling she might jump up all of a sudden and yell something.

Lou Davis sat behind Ebony, and her air space was being invaded by the black girl's hair. That day Miss Willbeck was droning on about some war or other, and I knew I'd better listen because this was the Big Year, the Year that would Decide Our Future, etc. etc., which we'd been hearing from parents and teachers for ages until we were either bored to tears or scared out of our tiny minds. Still, we had a good eight months before exams hit, so I figured I could waste a day or two staring at a black girl.

Except now it was Lou I was staring at. She was a petite girl with carefully shaped and sprayed hair in a fake shade of intense auburn. As I watched she casually removed a bottle of white correcting fluid from her pencil case. More than once I'd been on the receiving end of Lou's anger, expressed by flicking white blobs all over her victim. She belonged to a gang, the kind you didn't want to cross if you could help it.

Ebony tossed her head, and the back of her hair bounced up and down like a bundle of little snakes, right in Lou's face. Lou unscrewed the lid of the bottle. I wondered if Lou would go for the black girl's hair or just for the bright blue blazer. It would be easier to get that white stuff out of hair than off a school blazer.

"Star Smith!"

I nearly jumped out of my skin. "Yes, Miss?"

"I asked you a question, Star. What were some factors that contributed to the rise of Hitler after World War I? I'm sure you covered it last year; this is only review."

"Yes, Miss." I thought furiously and dredged up a couple of points from the bottom of my memory slush pit.

"Very good. Can anyone add to that?"

Miss Willbeck turned towards the other side of the room. I suspected that she saw Lou take out the bottle and was choosing to ignore it. A lot of teachers were like that with

Lou. She could get away with all kinds of things, like obvious make-up and bright nail varnish in spite of school rules, when the rest of us would be told off.

I kept my face turned towards the teacher but with my left eye I saw exactly what Lou was doing. She gave a tiny shrug like maybe she thought it was beneath her even to bother with this black creature, then she started painting over her long silver nails with the white fluid.

I thought it was dumb to paint over the silver with white, but then I saw she was drawing some kind of pattern on each nail.

It wasn't until she got to her thumb that I could see she was decorating each nail with two angular "s" letters crossing one another. A swastika. I had a feeling Lou wasn't painting swastikas on her nails just because we were about to study World War II.

LIFE ON CRAZY STREET

After school I walked home by myself as usual, but for some reason I decided to go through the park. Normally I walk about ten minutes out of my way to avoid it.

Just past the narrow park entrance stood a large clump of kids, talking and laughing. They had shed ties and blazers, and the girls had their grey skirts rolled up so high you could almost see their knickers. In the centre of the group were Lou and her boyfriend Matt; the rest of the gang clustered around them like bees on pollen. They blocked the park entrance every day, sharing cigarettes or joints and acting like they owned the world. The only sensible way to get past them was to put your head down and butt through the middle.

"Look at that, it's our Star!"

"Star light, Star bright–"

"Maybe I'll get to Hollywood, then I can be a Star!"

I just kept up my pace, not looking anyone in the eye, ignoring the silly taunts. At least they weren't in a shoving mood today. Please God, don't let them find out Star is only my middle name!

I made it through and started to cut across the grass. Behind me there was an unexpected sudden silence. In spite of myself, I hesitated and looked back.

The gang stood firm, not leaving an inch of space for anyone to enter the park. In spite of that, the black girl was forcing her way through their midst, head high and a look on her face that would scorch water. It was dead quiet until she popped out the other side and clumped away on her ridiculous high heels. Then they burst out with laughter and jeers. "You stupid Paki!" was the nicest thing I heard them say.

The black girl halted as if jerked back on a string. She whirled around and stared at them, one hand on her hip. She didn't look angry, just annoyed that they were wasting her time.

"Honey," she said in a syrupy accent, "if you think I'm a Paki, you better get glasses!"

I grinned. One point for Blackie! What kind of accent was that? I'd assumed she was Jamaican, but she sounded more like something out of an American film.

When I reached my street about five minutes later I could see our neighbour Mrs. Hinkeldorf leaning on her bedroom window sill, watching the kids walk home. If I hadn't seen her I probably would have called 999, because Mrs. H. was a woman of routine, and staring out the window at half past three each day was part of her daily pattern.

Mrs. H is from Germany, as she keeps reminding us, but I don't hold that against her country. Germany has moved on since Mrs. H's day. But God has a sense of humour, putting my family and Mrs. H in two halves of the same semi-detached house.

I turned into the paved area in front of our half. (We gave up on grass a long time ago.)

"Hello, you!"

Mrs. H. had opened her window and was leaning out. Her face framed in tight curls of short grey hair was just visible over the tops of the row of bushes she planted soon after we moved in, to divide our front garden from hers.

"My name is Star, Mrs. Hinkeldorf," I called back. She knew my name but she called all of us kids "you" and I figured telling her my name over and over was better than yelling "you" back at her.

"You, Star," she said, "there is a pair of shoes on your roof!"

"Oh right, Mrs. H. I've just left them out to dry in the sun."

Mrs. H. sputtered wordlessly and shut the window. I wondered how far she'd had to lean out of her window to see onto the little strip of roof over our front porch. I didn't know about the shoes but they were sure to belong to Cass, my older sister. She probably took them off before she climbed in our bedroom window in the middle of the night and forgot about them.

I stepped onto the porch and stuck my key in the front door. Our house looks fairly normal from outside, but I never let anyone I know cross the threshold. Maybe I lose friends that way, but I figure I'd lose even more if they saw the inside of the house and met my family. Better to stick to acquaintances than try for a close friend.

I stepped into the hall, kicking aside the pile of school bags and shoes dropped there by my three brothers. A din of excited barking echoed from the kitchen and a ball of black and white fur shot through the door and whacked into my legs, nearly knocking me over.

"Mopsy!" I yelled. "Get down!"

I tossed my own bag onto the heap and let our mongrel give me her version of a hug, complete with face bath. Wiping my face on my sleeve I went into the lounge where my three brothers sat with the curtains drawn, staring like zombies at a cartoon.

"I want the telly at four!" I said loudly.

Perse and Jase, the twins, didn't even register my presence. Six-year-old Baldy gave me his heart-melting grin before turning his eyes back to the flickering screen. Behind the sofa above their heads hung two large Greek masks, one smiling and the other crying, menacing in the dim wavering light.

I sighed. Why couldn't we have a painting of a woodland scene over our sofa like most normal people? Why did we have to have a mother who was so crazy about ancient Greece that she even named her children after heroes of mythology? And that was only tip of the iceberg, of all the reasons why I couldn't have friends over.

I wandered into the kitchen, which looked

like the set of a film about life in a houseful
of university students. The sink was stacked
with greasy pots and boxes of cereal were
still sitting out from breakfast. In other
words, for the Smith household, completely
normal.

I rummaged through the cupboards for
the chocolate spread, but couldn't find
it. I was sure there was a nearly full jar
somewhere. I finally located it underneath
a pile of pieces of cloth on the counter.
The jar was open and a chocolate-covered
knife rested on top. The bottom piece of
cloth had blobs of chocolate clinging to it,
but I figured that was Mum's problem, if
she wanted to leave bits of her work lying
around the kitchen.

There was one last clean saucer in the
dish cupboard. Mum had forgotten to buy
bread again, so I cut the blue spots off the
last piece and spread it with chocolate,
poured a glass of milk and headed upstairs.
Kicking open the door of the room I shared

with Cass, I squinted my eyes nearly shut and held my breath while I scooted through her part of the room as fast as I could without tripping over any scattered items of clothing.

My part of the bedroom was like the bottom of an L. I nudged aside the large sunflower bedspread I'd bought with my savings and hung as a curtain between the two sections of the room. As always, when I made it to my little kingdom, I let out my breath in a sigh of contentment. It was but clean and neat, my private pale blue sanctuary in the midst of chaos, like the eye at the centre of a hurricane.

I set saucer and glass on the nightstand and sat down on the bed, giving my hands a quick check for chocolate smears before I touched anything. Then I arranged the cushions and leaned back.

Adam's smiling face beamed at me from the photo frame as I reached for my snack, and I smiled back at him. He was a boy I knew from school – one I hoped to have a special friendship with someday. I'd taken the photo myself on a field trip last year. Even though the quality was poor the blue of his eyes still sparkled.

As if in echo, a pair of bright brown eyes topped by curly dark hair appeared around the corner of my curtain.

"What is it, Baldy?"

Normally I snapped like a vicious dog at any intrusion into my space, but Baldy could get away with it, so he was usually appointed messenger if anyone wanted me.

"Dad's asking where you are, Sissy."

"He knows where I am! I can be found in this very spot at this exact time after school every day." But I gulped the rest of my chocolate bread and went looking for Dad.

I found him in the study, which was a small room off the kitchen. It was meant for a laundry room, but Mum did her sewing there and the washer was out in the garage. The room was mostly taken up with sewing machine and a kaleidoscope of material scraps, with a tiny corner free for a small desk with telephone and computer. Dad was a travelling sales rep so he didn't use his desk that often anyway. Mum was gone at the moment, probably at some meeting to protest something, knowing her. I hoped the meeting wasn't at our school.

"How's my Star?"

"Fine, Dad."

"Good day at school?"

"Average. They're already trying to wind us up about our mock exams, though."

"I don't think you need to worry–you've always been a Star pupil!"

I smiled even though I'd heard it from him for the zillionth time. I guess it didn't bother me because I always felt like he meant it–like for him, I really was a star. Physically Dad was a small man with curly dark hair and bright brown eyes, just like Baldy. I was nearly as tall as he was, but I felt I'd always look up to him, if that made sense. Sometimes I wished—oh well, things were the way they were.

"You want something?" I asked.

"Just wondered if you'd seen this." He tossed me a copy of our local paper, and I shook my head.

The front-page headline screamed, "NEO-NAZI HATE. ARE OUR SCHOOLS NEXT?"

I scanned the article. It suggested without giving exact details that militant neo-Nazis were planning to infiltrate local schools by recruiting children at the school gates. It quoted an Anti-Nazi League spokesperson as saying that neo-Nazis would do everything possible to scare off black people.

"But we don't even have any black people around here," I said, although just then the image of Ebony popped into my mind. "Or only a few."

Dad's eyes clouded over. "You know that doesn't mean just people whose skin is dark. It means anyone who isn't of pure white race.

"Have you noticed anything like that going on outside your school?" he asked. "Anyone passing out leaflets or trying to talk to the kids as they leave?"

"No, I haven't, and I'm sure I would have seen it. Don't worry about it."

He smiled and gave a little shrug, then turned back to his computer.

I knew why Dad was worried. It had to do with the Family Secret. But I wasn't going to think about that now. I was going to go back up to my peaceful haven and chill out.

Wrong! Just as I started up the stairs the front door flew open, crashing into the wall. Cass was home early.

THE ROCK STARTS TO ROLL

"Hi, everybody!" Cass yelled at the top of her lungs, in spite of the fact that I was standing three feet away from her.

She was still blonde which was how she left the house that morning, so she'd had a good day. On bad days at the hair salon where she was a trainee and hair-washer, she'd usually spray on some other colour during her lunch break. Her hair stood out in feathery spikes all around her head, which I thought made her face look even rounder. Add to that a ton of black eyeliner, black clothes and so much jewellery that she clanked when she breathed, and there you have my older sister!

At college, Cass was training to be a hairdresser. In life, she was training to be noticed, and doing a good job of it. Sometimes I couldn't believe we came from the same parents and were only a year apart in age. I guess I just didn't want to admit it.

"You left your shoes on the roof last night," I said. "You better bring them in or Mrs. Hinkeldorf will have a fit. I told her they were mine, but I'm not bringing them in for you."

"Thanks, luv," she beamed at me. "I'll return the favour some day, when you go out with your Adam!"

"Cass," I said, "he is not my Adam—I just happen to have a photo of him! And if we ever do go out, I'll have enough sense to let myself in the front door with my key, instead of being hoisted up onto the roof!"

"I've got some time, I could do your hair," she offered, ignoring my comment.

"No, thanks— not today!" I said quickly.

I raced upstairs, my emotions on a low boil. Why did she always think she had to mother me? "Luv" indeed! I was getting so fed up with her acting like the worldly wise older sister. There was no need for her to poke and pry into my personal life, either! I didn't remember mentioning anything about Adam–she must have been snooping around and seen the photo.

She didn't have to climb in at the window last night– Mum and Dad probably wouldn't have made a fuss if she'd rung the bell, no matter what time it was. But that was Cass for you. She'd joined a local drama group recently and I thought it was making her even worse.

Back in my room, I glanced in the mirror over my dresser. My hair probably did need help. It was a pathetic dull colour somewhere between brown and blonde and hung straight and limp, except where it frizzed over my forehead. It didn't do a thing for my thin pale face. Maybe I should get Cass to curl it and dye it red or something, but I just wasn't that adventurous.

I tried to recapture the peace of my sanctuary, but it had gone for good. I

turned up my radio as loud as it would go,
flopped down on my bed and did my best to
concentrate on some homework.

* * *

We were reminded first thing at school
the next day that our parents were invited
that night for Open Evening. I'd completely
forgotten, and my emotions took a roller-
coaster ride downwards. I knew my whole
family would come, probably even Cass.
There was no way I could avoid being seen
with them, since I was on the list of greeters.

I was leaving the assistant Head's
office after getting our instructions for the
evening, when I passed the black girl on her
way in. Her head was cocked to one side
and her high cheekbones looked like they
were chiselled out of chocolate. I got a clue
as to why she was sent there when I noticed
how short her skirt was rolled up, and she
hadn't even bothered to let it back down to
see the assistant Head. Was she trying to get
sent home?

"Hi, Star," someone said in my ear.

"Oh... hi," I replied. My heart slowed nearly to cardiac arrest and beads of sweat broke out on my upper lip. It was Adam, who fell in step with me. He grinned down at me, his straight brown hair falling over one eye the way it always did. I felt all watery inside whenever his hair did that.

I turned my head and pretended to cough. Actually I was wiping the sweat off my lip. Then I gave him a big smile back. We didn't have any lessons together so getting to see him up close was something special.

"What do you think of the Tall Black One?" he asked, with a nod towards the office where Ebony had just gone inside.

"She's hopeless, isn't she?" I said with a laugh. "Did you see her skirt just now?"

"Maybe we'll be lucky and she'll get herself expelled," Adam said.

"Maybe," I said, smiling up at him. At that point he could have said anything and I would have agreed.

"I don't see you very often," he said, echoing my own thoughts. "Are you coming tonight?"

"Have to–I'm one of the greeters."

"I'm selling plants for business studies. Well, see you tonight," he said, as he turned away to head for his lesson.

See you tonight, see you tonight, I heard his voice say over and over as I walked in a daze outside and down the path towards the languages building. It was a cool but sunny autumn day and the leaves were starting to turn. Actually it could have been raining little puppies for all I cared. Adam noticed me! He actually wanted to spend time with me!

But then I remembered that my whole family would be there tonight as well. An evil fate might decide that the moment at which Adam saw me would be the exact time that the Smith clan showed up. So far I didn't think he connected me with Cass, who had earned quite a reputation when she was at our school. I wanted to keep it that way.

* * *

That night my worst fears about Open Evening were confirmed. I stood with several other pupils inside the school entrance, dressed in full uniform, handing out blue leaflets to arriving parents.

It wasn't long before my mum appeared, trailing family members behind her like a colourful mother goose with wildly assorted goslings. I cringed when I saw she was wearing one of her own creations, an oversized hot pink sweatshirt decorated with ribbons and fake jewels. She had a good business, decorating and selling T-shirts and sweatshirts, and her stuff was high quality, but it was very attention-getting. The more so because Mum wasn't exactly slender and her long wavy hair looked like something left out in the rain after the Sixties.

Why did the sight of my family all together make me want to throw up? I was about to squinch my eyes shut, hoping they'd all disappear without greeting me, when I saw the Headmaster, Mr. Parkson, come out of his office to my right.

"Mr. Parkson!" Mum boomed over the crowd. She shouldered her way towards him, giving frantic hand waves for her brood to follow her.

They all met up next to my right elbow, and I was too hemmed in to escape.

"Lovely to see you, Mrs. Smith," Mr. Parkson said with a professional smile. Even with over a thousand pupils in his school, I was not surprised that he knew my mother by name.

"You know my husband, Harold," she said, pushing Dad slightly forward so that he would shake Mr. Parkson's hand. Dad did, looking earnest and faintly embarrassed. "And our twins, Perseus and Jason."

Perse and Jase, both wallowing in their new huge blue blazers like all the year seven kids, shook hands with the Headmaster. It was too bad the school governors always voted for uniforms instead of letting us wear normal clothes. You'd think they would at least allow sweatshirts instead of blazers, but no, everything was strictly regulated at our school: full uniform, skirts a decent length, no jewellery, make-up or nail varnish.

"We're very glad to have you boys join us this year," Mr. Parkson said. There was a slight pause and I thought he might be wondering if these two, with their curly ginger hair and innocent-looking blue eyes, would turn out to be like Cass or like me.

"And we'll have another coming your way in a few years. This is our little Baldur," Mum said, and Baldy stuck out his hand and grinned at the Head. Mr. Parkson's eyes widened slightly when he heard Baldy's name.

"And Cassandra," Mum went on, giving Cass a jerk forwards that set off a round of jangling as bracelets and earrings collided with each other.

"Cassandra, lovely to see you. How are

things at college?"

As Cass gave Mr. Parkson her reply I was trying to make myself small and disappear, but a firm hand grabbed my shoulder.

"And of course, our An– our Star," Mum concluded, serving me up like dessert at the end of a feast. At least she was sticking to our agreement to use my middle name.

It was at that moment that I saw Adam enter the hall and make his way in our direction. Our eyes met, and he raised a hand and smiled. I saw the smile fade slightly as he took in the group around me and the fact that Mum was clutching my elbow with an air of ownership.

"One of our outstanding pupils," Mr. Parkson said, smiling at me. "Well," he added with the sudden air of a man with things to attend to, "if you'll excuse me... I hope you enjoy the evening!"

"Star," Mum said to me as Mr. Parkson vanished, "tell us where everything is!" Adam had disappeared into the Hall, which was where the sales stands were.

"It's all in the leaflet, Mum." Honestly, you'd think the woman couldn't read! Did parents take stupid pills with their breakfast vitamins?

"I know, but you could give us an idea of where to start—"

People walking past us all turned and stared. I could feel my cheeks glowing hot and red. Suddenly there was a tug at my sleeve.

"Star! Could I have a word?"

It was my P.E. teacher, Miss Cleeves. She looked odd in a dress instead of jogging suit and she seemed flustered.

"It's Katie— she's taken ill, and I've no one else who can do the badminton demonstration. Do you have your P.E. kit here?"

I nodded. "It's in my locker."

"Would you be willing to help? I think there are enough greeters."

Would I! Anything to vanish from the

presence of my weird family! Without bothering to say goodbye I tossed my remaining leaflets to one of the other greeters and followed Miss Cleeves quickly to the gym.

Helping Miss Cleeves with the badminton display was a small thing. It was something I didn't mind doing because I like badminton, and it got me out of reach of my family. But I didn't realise that something very small that you do can have far-reaching consequences, like giving a rock a slight shove over the edge of a canyon, never thinking it will build up so much speed and force all on its own.

BLACKIE AND WHITEY

At the locker room I changed quickly, grabbed a racquet and dashed onto the gym floor, passing the trampoline display to reach the badminton court at the far end. Lots of parents and kids were milling around, clapping every time someone turned a flip in the air. It hadn't occurred to me to wonder who my opponent in badminton would be, but then I saw someone tall and black in blue and white gym clothes.

I didn't want to play with her! That was my first reaction, and it made me feel a little guilty. But then I told myself it had nothing to do with her colour– it was just that she wouldn't play very well and we'd both look stupid.

Ebony stood straight and scornful, giving a slight nod of greeting when I stepped onto the court. She'd tied her hair up on the top of her head so it looked like a small brown shrub, which nodded when she did. Her eyes glimmered like she was in a mood with me for some reason. Maybe she didn't want to play with a white girl– but she was out of luck, since that's all our school had to offer!

I took the first serve and several families wandered down to our side of the gym to watch. To my surprise we were evenly matched, and I think of myself as a fairly good player. So I had to concentrate hard, learning to guess where the black girl would send the shuttlecock next. She had me leaping back and forth all over the court.

Out of one corner of my eye I was checking to see if my family had worked out where I was. Any minute now they'd probably show up and start cheering, which was something I wanted to avoid. I jumped and hit with all my skill as if that would get me out sooner, when actually I knew we were here for thirty minutes, no matter how well or poorly I played.

It occurred to me that I hadn't seen any black parents on the sidelines. Ebony was lucky, but maybe her parents would show up at the same time as mine, and then everyone would stare at hers instead. I found myself hoping for that.

We were both sweating like pigs by now. The haughty glare on Ebony's face was etched in brown stone, and I could feel my temper rise to the challenge. It would have been the moment to raise our swords and shout, "To the death!"– except that we were just two schoolgirls in short blue pleated skirts, wielding little racquets.

Just as I was thinking that I heard sniggers coming from the sidelines and a muttered phrase. I only caught the words "Blackie and Whitey" but my concentration slipped and I lost the point. I glanced back and saw a cluster of kids standing behind me. I recognized Matt the gang leader and some of his friends, but I couldn't tell who had said it.

Something inside me twinged, like someone had stuck a needle in the centre of my chest. Come on, come on you idiot! I silently scolded myself. Why would I let a little thing like that bother me? I'd called Ebony "Blackie" myself, and my own whiteness couldn't be argued.

I lost that game but by the end of the 30 minutes I was one game ahead– maybe only because I was just a hair faster on the court than Ebony. She loped over to my side and we touched our dripping palms together while the parents clapped. My family hadn't shown up so I was feeling chuffed.

"Good game!" I said.

"Yeah." A corner of Ebony's mouth crimped upwards. It wasn't a smile but at least she didn't look angry that I'd won.

One of the families standing on the sidelines stepped forward and surrounded Ebony, telling her how well she played. The haughty mask slipped back into place and she greeted them in an irritated tone.

I watched, puzzled, as they moved off together. The parents and a couple of young children were all white and didn't sound American. Maybe Ebony was just staying with them temporarily, or maybe they had taken her in as a foster child. But then why was she so rude to them? That made it look like they really were her own family.

* * *

I saw Ebony in drama class the day after. She struck me as being an alien life form and that made me wish I could find out more about her.

Our drama teacher, Mrs. O'Brien, had us doing "trust exercises". She was small and energetic, the kind of teacher who made everything so interesting you forgot you were learning something at the same time.

"All right, class," she said, "circle up!"

We knew what to do because we'd begun last year with the same exercises. The point was to build up teamwork before we started working together on the autumn play.

Everyone clustered together in the centre of the room, making a close circle. Ebony hung back a little because she hadn't been there when we did this before.

"Come on!" I urged her, waving her to stand next to me on the left. She shrugged and moved into place.

"Now turn to the right," Mrs. O'Brien commanded, "and tighten your circle!"

We turned so that each person was jammed up behind the person on their right.

"On the count of three, I want everybody to sit. One– two– three– sit!"

We all let ourselves go slowly backwards into a sitting position. There was some laughing and a few shrieks as small girls were nearly squashed by hulking boys, but we knew from past experience that we could do it if we concentrated on being a team.

Of course Ebony didn't know that. I had to remind myself she was new after she stood up suddenly and I plunged to the floor.

"What on earth are y'all doing?" she demanded, leaning over me and scowling as if it was all my fault. Her hair stuck out in all directions like she'd just had a major electric shock.

Our whole section of the circle had collapsed and bodies were strewn everywhere. That was part of the fun and we were all laughing except Lou, who had been right behind Ebony when she stood up. Lou had hit the floor with force and her eyes were turned on the black girl like two fiery blue lasers. I laughed even harder when I saw Lou's perfect hair was rumpled in the fall and now looked almost as wild as Ebony's.

"We're meant to sit down on each other's laps," I explained to Ebony. "It works, if we all do it at once."

"Well, it's dumb!" she replied loudly.

Mrs. O'Brien just smiled and went on helping people to their feet and getting the circle back in shape. But it did make

me wonder about Ebony. She seemed to
be going out of her way to be difficult.
I guessed she'd be in real trouble with
somebody soon– Lou and the gang, if no
one else. I felt kind of protective of her, just
because we'd played badminton together.

I didn't have to wait long to see my
prophecy fulfilled.

After school I decided to walk through
the park instead of doing the extra minutes
to avoid the gang. I had a lot of homework
that day and figured I could get a good
chunk of it done before supper. Okay, so
I am a bit of a swot. I don't like putting
everything off to the last minute.

I tried to collect my things and get down
to the park before the gang had a chance
to congregate. But my maths teacher
always thinks whatever he's saying is more
important than the end-of-school bell, so I
was late. It just so happened that Ebony was
right in front of me when I stepped through
the park entrance.

Already there were about twenty of them there in their usual pose, jammed together in a tight clan with cigarettes lit. The instant Ebony appeared there was a collective stiffening. Lou's eyes narrowed to cobalt blue slits which she turned on Matt, signalling him to do something.

Matt wore his hair as close to shaved as he could without being sent home from school. He seemed to have rings and studs piercing every available space from the neck up. He took them out before school and stuck them back in as soon as he left each day.

"Well, look here," he called out, his voice dripping with amusement, "it's Blackie and Whitey! You two are really friendly these days."

As soon as I heard him say that I slowed down and let Ebony get ahead of me. No way was I going to be thought of as her friend! The black girl didn't even glance at me. She probably felt the same. She just snorted through her nose like a horse and began to shove her way through the gang.

They pressed in even tighter, and she pushed abruptly at the kids standing closest to her. There was a pause, then a sudden burst of laughter. I saw a little brown hole appear on the side of Ebony's blue blazer, right near the shoulder where it would be most visible.

I couldn't believe they'd had the nerve to poke her with a fag on her new blazer! That made me so angry I didn't stop to think about consequences. I leaped forward and grabbed her arm, pulling her away from the centre of the gang and around to the side where we could force our way past.

That brought more laughter and taunts like "Uh-oh, look out everybody, Blackie's got protection!"

I continued to clutch Ebony's arm, but as we left the gang behind she jerked it away.

"I don't need your help, white girl!" she said, storming off and leaving me standing there feeling like an absolute fool.

MY SISTER, THE DISASTER ZONE!

I stood there for only as long as it took me to decide that I wasn't going home after all. Laughter from the gang drifted after me as I strode up the grassy hill in the opposite direction from Ebony, heading for the centre of town.

I decided to drop in on Cass at work with a vague idea of telling her my troubles, even though I never did. Anything was better than going home right now to a messy house full of freaks.

When I pushed on the glass door at the hairdressers' a cloud of damp air escaped, hitting my nose and eyes with a blast of perfumed sprays and perm solution. There were posh salons in our town, but this wasn't one of them. It had lilac ruffled curtains in the window and was frequented by little old ladies. I never could figure out

why Cass always seemed to be so popular
with the OAPs but even as a lowly trainee
she had her regulars who got very cross if
she was away.

The shop owner was working on a lady
who was almost bald, her hair was so thin.
What hair she had was dyed a bluish silver. I
didn't see Cass among the other stylists, but
the owner caught sight of me and nodded
towards the back.

There was a room at the rear where
the stylists had their breaks. I found Cass
standing at the mirror over a sink, her
expression like a round smiley face gone sad.
Chunks of her hair were sprayed a bright
auburn, and she was working with a can of
spray colour to make the ends a glowing
purple.

"What happened?" I blurted out,
forgetting my own troubles for the moment.
Judging from the three-tone hair this was a
very bad day for my older sister.

Cass glanced in the mirror at me, then

looked back to her handiwork. She puckered her face with concentration and gave a few shots from the spray can, then fluffed her hair with her fingers to see the effect. All of a sudden I noticed a fat tear rolling down one side of her face.

"Cass, what is it?" I demanded, fear squeezing my heart. I couldn't remember the last time I'd seen her cry, except for dramatic effect. This looked real.

She looked at me and then gave a big sniff, flopped down on a nearby sofa and burst into tears. I found a box of tissues and tossed it to her and sat beside her while she mopped up rivers of black mascara.

"Oh, Sis," she said finally when she could speak. "Look at this!"

She jumped up and went into the loo, then came out with something in her hand. She stuck it in front of my face, but it didn't mean anything to me. It was a white plastic tube with a pink dot on the side. "What is it?"

She stared at me blankly for a second, then shook her head.

"You are so naive!" she exclaimed. "It's a pregnancy test."

I could feel the blood drain from my face.

She nodded. "That's right. I'm pregnant." She sat back down and the tears started to flow again. I patted her shoulder, trying to make her feel better but knowing with a sinking feeling that it wouldn't help much.

"Are you sure? Maybe the test made a mistake."

Cass shook her head, her long earrings brushing her shoulders.

"I missed my period, which I never do. And I don't think these tests are ever wrong. You wee on this little stick, and if there's a pink dot in the window, that's it."

"What are you going to do? Mum and Dad will go spare!"

"Yeh, I know. You've got to help me!"

"What do you mean?"

"Star," she said, leaning close and

clutching my arm, "you've got to tell them!
You could tell them when I'm out of the
house and then I could come in after they've
calmed down a bit."

"I don't think so!" I said. "It's not fair to
ask me that. But I'll be with you when you
tell them, if you want."

Cass nodded, looking mournful.

"I don't know what I'll do," she added,
blotting her face with soggy tissue. "I don't
think Paul is going to be very happy about
this– he's hoping to go to university."

"Don't you two use birth control?" I
asked, then blushed at the thought of what
we were discussing.

Cass shrugged. "Most of the time."

I looked at her and she looked at me and
then the silly side of her remark struck us
both, and we burst out in hysterical giggles.
It wasn't funny though– we were just letting
off steam.

'Oh, God, oh, God,' I kept thinking over
and over as I trudged back through the park

towards home. Was I praying? I don't know.
I didn't have much use for God before now,
and I wasn't even sure if he was there. If he
was, what did I expect him to do– wave a
magic wand over Cass and make the baby
disappear?

It wasn't until I passed the place
where the gang always stood that I
even remembered why I'd gone to the
hairdressers' in the first place. My own
problems seemed pale and flabby, compared
to what was about to strike our family. The
park was deserted now except for a couple
of people with dogs. The gang had gone
back to whatever slimy cave they hid in
until the next day. I guess really they all had
homes, but I couldn't picture it.

I tried for a minute to picture Ebony's
home as well, but I couldn't get anything
into focus. Suddenly I was furious as I
thought of how rude she'd been with her
"white girl" comment. Didn't she realise
how much I was risking, even pretending

to be her friend in front of the gang? You'd have thought she'd be more grateful! The sensible thing would have been to make up my mind to avoid her from then on, but for some reason I didn't do that.

When I reached our house I glanced up out of habit, but no Mrs. Hinkeldorf. I was too late to give her the pleasure of staring at me. Five o'clock already; she probably vacuumed her ceilings at that hour every day.

I let myself in, shielding my tights from Mopsy's friendly attack as I ran up the stairs to my room. Moving through Cass's area I really looked at her stuff for the first time in a while. The walls were painted bright yellow and stuck with lots of cheery travel posters. The floor and unmade bed were strewn with clothes, mostly black. The top of her dresser was invisible under a mountain of cheap jewellery, cosmetics and dirty hairbrushes.

But there was one shelf on the wall which was tidy. It must have been her childhood memento shelf because it held an orderly stack of books like Dr. Seuss and Beatrix Potter, several souvenir dolls from different countries and a misshapen pottery bowl she'd made at junior school.

I was usually so busy staying out of Cass's way that I didn't bother getting to know her. The shelf of little mementos made me sad. She was about to have to leave her childhood behind for good.

Instead of just hiding in my retreat I thought I'd clean up the kitchen a bit, maybe start some food going. I hoped I could improve the atmosphere so Cass's announcement that evening would be cushioned, as far as that might be possible.

As I scrubbed some encrusted pans that had sat in the kitchen sink since the night before, I played the scene in advance. I could imagine the faces around the supper table when Cass dropped her bombshell: Baldy dirt-smudged as usual, probably smiling because he didn't understand what was happening; the twins excited, thinking they'd be able to play with the baby like one of their pet guinea pigs; Dad sad, disappointed in Cass but probably supportive; Mum? I couldn't predict her reaction. She'd either burst out laughing or screaming.

I jabbed a frying pan with the scrubber. It's her fault! I fumed. She didn't even care what kind of trouble we get in. Maybe I should start shoplifting or something! Then she'd notice what a rotten mother she'd been. I was sure she'd never had a serious mother-daughter talk with Cass. At least, she hadn't with me.

"Star! What a pleasant surprise!"

Mum's voice in my ear made me jump guiltily. She was wearing turquoise today, her sweatshirt accented with swirls of metallic paint around the neckline. The bright colours made the streaks of grey in her long hair stand out. If she was going to dress like that, I wished she'd stay at home so no one could see her.

"Yeh, I got tired of looking at all this," I replied. "I can start supper too, if you want."

"No, I'll do that– you just keep on there. And thanks!"

Mum beamed at me and then turned to get some things out of the fridge. I felt squirmy over the thought that my helpfulness was obviously such a rare thing, and even now I was only pitching in because of trying to make things easier for Cass.

Before long Cass and Dad were home and we were all sitting down to a meal of fried eggs and chips. We didn't always eat together, only if everyone happened to be around, and I shot Cass a meaning glance several times. If she wanted to make her announcement to the whole family, this was the time to do it. She kept avoiding my eyes. I think Dad noticed she seemed subdued, but everyone else was talking at once the way they usually did.

Cass glanced at me when no one was

looking and I mouthed silently "Tell them!" But she shook her head and started rearranging the food on her plate with her knife and fork. Everyone was finished and she had half her eggs and most of the fries left.

Mum started to clear the table and Cass jumped up and tipped her food into Mopsy's dish when Mum's back was turned. Then she ran out of the room and up the stairs. I strained to listen above the clatter of dishes and the dog's happy slurping sounds and heard faint throwing-up noises coming from the upstairs loo.

"What's wrong with Cass?" Dad asked me.

I shrugged at him. "I've got a lot of homework," I said, leaving the table quickly before he quizzed me any further. I didn't like lying and I was not going to let my sister dump her responsibility onto me!

TRUSTING IS TRICKY

Radio One was turned up loud so I wouldn't have to think. I had an art project due the next day; it was a pastel drawing of reflective surfaces that just needed a few last highlights.

I sat on the floor beside my bed with the drawing in front of me and got out my pastels. My hand was shaking. The drawing wasn't very good because I'm not a creative person, but I didn't want to ruin something I'd already spent hours on.

After a minute I put my pastels away. I'd have to finish it before school tomorrow. I lay down on the bed, snuggled up on my cushions with my duvet around my legs and let the sounds of music roll over me, trying to make my brain go numb, but it refused to.

What would Mum and Dad do when they found out about Cass? Would she marry

Paul, not marry him but keep the baby, have an abortion? If she did keep it, where would it sleep? My mind veered away from the obvious answer to that one.

I leaped off the bed and tore back my curtain. Cass was curled up on her bed too, staring into space while her radio played quiet background music. Funny, you'd have thought she would be out with Paul. Maybe she just couldn't face him yet.

"Cass, you have to tell them!"

She glanced up at me blankly as if wondering who I was.

"It's me, your sister! I am not going to put up with dragging this thing out. Let's go down there now. I'll go with you."

Cass chewed on her lower lip for a moment, then nodded. "Okay," she said with a giant sigh. "You're right, it'll just be worse, the longer I wait."

"Believe me, they'll figure it out pretty soon if you keep on hurling your dinner. Better to tell them before they start asking."

The boys were already in their rooms, settling down for the night. The twins' light was still on, so I flicked it off and told them goodnight on our way down the stairs. I also shut their door tightly, an automatic reflex to keep the zoo-like smells from drifting through the house. I'd warned Mum not to let them have two of anything, but there were seventeen guinea pigs at last count.

Cass and I found Mum and Dad in their bedroom, in the room next to the kitchen that was probably meant for dining. They both liked to read in bed so they were already propped up on their pillows, books in hand. Each of their nightstands was spilling over with library books, newspapers and magazines.

"Hi, girls," Mum said cheerily, just glancing up briefly from her book. Dad's forehead creased in a worried frown and he turned his book face down on the covers. He had enough sense to know this wasn't a social call.

Cass just stood there, her arms crossed tightly over her stomach like she was protecting the new little life growing there from possible attack.

Even Mum put her book down now, vaguely aware something was wrong.

It was beginning to look like we'd be there to the middle of next week if I didn't start things rolling. "Cass has something to tell you," I said breathlessly.

She took a deep breath, but her voice came out tiny, like a little kid. "Mum, Dad– I– Paul and I– well, we weren't always careful like we should have been and I know you're going to go spare and I wouldn't blame you if you hate me and I just don't know what to do!" Then she burst into tears.

It got very quiet in the room. Mum and Dad took on the stony look of ancient statues. They could have been carved in marble and placed in a museum in the next century, labelled Parents Receiving News of Daughter's Pregnancy. Then Dad's face kind of crumpled into disappointed sadness, just as I'd predicted.

But Mum surprised me. She squared her shoulders and flung back the covers to jump up and put her arms around Cass. "These things happen," she said, with only a small catch in her voice. Probably she was holding back on her true feelings. Or maybe she didn't have feelings. I'd suspected that for a long time.

"Oh, Mum!" Cass wailed, and she sobbed with relief on Mum's shoulder. Dad got up too to join them, and I left the room quietly. They didn't need me now.

I hid in the bathroom. Since it was the only bathroom in the house it didn't have much to recommend it– no danger of it ever appearing in Beautiful Homes magazine, or anything. As usual it was a jungle of damp towels and little boys' underwear. Its only good feature was the lock on the door.

I ran warm water into the tub, threw in some bath crystals (which for obvious reasons I keep under lock and key in my room) and let myself in for a good soak.

As I lay there gazing at the patterns of mould between the dark green tiles it hit me how much I wished I had a friend I could ring up right now, tell the whole thing to. I couldn't chat about all this to just anyone, but it would have been nice to have one close friend, somebody I could trust. I leafed through my mental list of acquaintances, but I just couldn't come up with anyone I would dare bring into my home, or entrust with secrets like the thing with Cass or the other big one our family never mentioned.

* * *

Ebony was one person I didn't want to see the next day, but I couldn't avoid her since we had drama together. I was still annoyed about her "white girl" comment. She didn't have so many friends that she could afford to waste any! Not that I wanted to be her friend, anyway.

The problem with doing trust exercises

like the ones in drama class is that you have
to trust the other people, or they don't work.
I didn't trust Lou, or Matt the gang leader,
who was also in our group, as well as several
of his slaves. Now I didn't trust Ebony. After
the way she acted yesterday, I didn't have
any idea what she'd do next.

And today's exercises could be dangerous,
if someone wasn't trustworthy. Mrs. O'Brien
should have sensed the atmosphere in the
classroom.

The day was cold and blustery, in the
unpredictable way of autumn weather.
Several kids from the gang came into the
classroom still wearing their jackets.

"Take your coats off, please," said Mrs.
O'Brien.

"But, Miss, it's cold in here," Lou argued.

"Yeh, we're really freezing," one of the
gang boys said. Matt said nothing but just
rocked back in his chair with a grin on his
face, like he knew he was the one with all the
power here.

"Very well, then," said Mrs. O'B., her eyes snapping angrily, "we'll turn the radiators up."

There were muffled groans from the rest of us, because it was already warm enough, and we didn't need a tropical atmosphere. Trust exercises involved physical contact, and who wanted to touch sweaty bodies?

Mrs. O'Brien marched across the room and wrenched the radiator knob open full blast.

"There. Now will you please all remove your coats."

At the barest nod from Matt all the gang members peeled off their coats. I wondered what it was about him that made them all grovel and do his slightest bidding. He seemed pretty average to me, except for the nearly shaved head and all the holes for his rings and studs. Did he threaten to break their legs or beat up their grannies? The bizarre thing was that they didn't seem to resent his authority.

The first exercises weren't so bad. Four people on each side stood facing one another, arms held out, and then one person ran and dived into the waiting arms. Even if one or two kids "accidentally" let their arms drop, you could manage to break your own fall.

I was one of the catchers for that round. Ebony was standing across from me and I tried glaring at her, but I might as well have been invisible. She acted like she didn't even remember me. Maybe all white people looked alike to her.

On the next exercise Mrs. O'Brien picked me to fall off a table backwards into the waiting arms of four people. My pulse rate shot up when I saw who they were: Lou, Matt, another gang girl, and Ebony.

Standing on the table with my back to them I heard Matt mutter, "Catch your friend, Blackie." The gang kids wouldn't hesitate to drop me as long as it looked accidental, and I figured Ebony would just stand there and let it happen. I was wondering how severe my injuries would be when Mrs. O'Brien ordered "Fall now!"

I closed my eyes and because I couldn't think of a way to get out of it, I fell.

Scuffling sounds and yells— I didn't take in much because it happened so fast. I opened my eyes and saw I was on the floor, but Ebony was beneath me. She must have fallen or been dragged down in such a way that she hit the floor first, protecting my fall. The other three catchers were making fake "Sorry!" noises but Mrs. O'Brien wasn't fooled. The bell went then, and she motioned angrily for them to follow her, probably to the Head's office.

"Are you hurt?" I shoved over so Ebony could get up.

She was lying on her back looking winded, but she shook her head.

"Sorry for falling on you," I said. "I don't know how that happened, but I'm just glad I didn't land on my head!"

Ebony shrugged. "I knew they had it in for you."

So she did it on purpose! I broke out in a big smile and started to ask her if we could walk home together, when someone called my name from the doorway.

"Star! I've been looking for you."

It was Adam. I jumped up and brushed the dust off my skirt, hoping my hair wasn't a total mess.

"Why don't you walk to town with me after school?" he asked. "I need some graph paper."

"Yeh, why not," I replied. I grabbed my bag and followed him out the door, not even thinking to say goodbye to Ebony.

"What were you doing with her?" he asked as we left the room.

I glanced back at Ebony. She was busy collecting her books, apparently not listening to us, but I could see the brown of her cheeks was overlaid with a tinge of red.

WELCOME TO THE ASYLUM!

"I wasn't doing anything with her," I said
to Adam as we walked into town. I tried to
explain how the black girl had thrown herself
to the floor to keep me from being injured.

Adam looked down at me with concern
in his blue eyes. My heart began to do a
little hip-hop. I would have done anything to
make him keep looking at me like that.

"It's just that people will get the wrong
idea about you," he said, "if they keep on
seeing you hanging around with coloureds."

That remark hit me in the face like a wet
dishcloth. A lot of images started tossing
around in my mind: Ebony's haughty sneer
when she called me "white girl"; the worry
in Dad's eyes over neo-Nazis; the menacing
smile on the face of Matt, the gang leader.

The sickening thing was, Adam was right.
Some people would "get the wrong idea" if

I spent any more time with Ebony. It was clear Adam included himself in that. And he was one person in the school I really wanted to think well of me. Probably the best thing would be to ignore Ebony from now on.

I got home just in time to experience a drama involving Mrs. Hinkeldorf and her disgraceful neighbours, the Smith family. It was too late for her to be at the window but as I turned into our drive I heard muffled shrieks coming from her side of the hedge.

Just as I was about to go check it out Mrs. H. popped around the end of the drive like a jack-in-the-box. She was shaking and babbling something in German so I put my hand on her arm to steady her.

"Mrs. Hinkeldorf, what is it?" I asked.

For a few seconds her mouth opened and shut like she was having trouble getting it to switch to English.

"Those boys!" she exclaimed, when she could speak. "I am cleaning the shower, and there it is! On the curtain rod! I nearly touch it!"

It started to make sense. I ran over to our front door, opened it and stuck my head in.

"Hey!" I yelled. "Have you boys lost Fred?"

Feet thundered upstairs accompanied by excited barks from Mopsy. Shouts of dismay from the upper regions. Conclusion: Fred was missing. Fred was the twins' boa constrictor, and it didn't take Sherlock Holmes to deduce that he could be found wrapped around the shower curtain rod in Mrs. Hinkeldorf's house.

I ordered the boys next door and brought Mrs. H. into our kitchen, shutting the door so she wouldn't see Fred being carried back upstairs to his aquarium. For a boa he was pretty small, only three feet long, but still not something you want to meet in your shower.

"Would you like a cup of tea, Mrs. Hinkeldorf?" I asked. I didn't even know if Germans drank tea, but what could it hurt?

She nodded, still trembling slightly. Her

face was almost the same grey as her short permed hair. I made mugs of tea for both of us and sat down with her at the kitchen table. She looked suspiciously at the chair seat before lowering herself into it. In our house, not a bad idea.

We drank in silence for a while.

"I am sorry," Mrs. H. said after a bit. "Sometimes it is very difficult for me, living next to your family. I know that children like to do strange things, but snakes...." She shuddered. "It should not be allowed! There should be laws about such things!"

"I'll try to make the boys be more careful," I said. Fat chance! I could only hope next time Fred got out, he didn't end up in her bed.

And what on earth would she say when she found out what Cass had been up to? Of course, if she had an abortion, no one would know. Cass was the motherly type, though, and I couldn't quite picture her killing off her baby. I'd always assumed abortion was perfectly okay, but now I began to wonder.

* * *

I found myself hovering around the small study later that evening. Mum and Dad were both there; Dad was on the computer and Mum was finishing off a stack of colourful sweatshirts. Cass was out with Paul. He was an okay guy but I wonder how he'd handle knowing he was a father.

"Why don't you give me a hand?" Mum asked.

These particular sweatshirts had to be carefully clipped on the front to reveal a pattern already sewn on the reverse. Normally she didn't ask me to help and I didn't offer. It was detailed work and she knew I wasn't very quick at it like she and Cass were, but I could manage it if I concentrated.

I pulled up a chair, took the extra pair of scissors and began to clip carefully around the stitching on a purple sweatshirt. I kind of wished Mum wasn't there because I wanted to talk some things over with Dad. I wondered if they had spoken to Cass about the baby. Also, I was confused about Ebony. It made sense to ignore her but I couldn't make myself feel totally at ease about that.

The three of us worked in silence for a while. Mum was starting on a third sweatshirt and I was still on my first. She seemed a lot more quiet than usual but I put it down to the whole business with Cass.

Finally Dad turned off the computer and wheeled around in his chair.

"Did you have a good day in school, luv?" he asked.

For a moment I just kept my head down and concentrated on my work. "Not exactly," I said finally. I should have just lied and said yes, because I didn't want to get into it with Mum sitting there.

Mum looked up with a startled expression on her face.

"What happened?" she asked. "I've never known you to have a bad day!"

That made me furious. Maybe she thought of me as always having good days at school, just because I got good marks. When did she ever bother to find out?

"Well, if you really want to know," I said indignantly, "I almost fell on my head. You would have had to take me to casualty if this black girl hadn't decided to break my fall." I explained the whole scene, including how the gang was out to get me, because they thought I was friends with Ebony.

Dad listened carefully, and I could tell he was picturing the whole thing from different points of view: mine, Ebony's, the gang members. He had a knack for doing that, for backing off from a situation and seeing it from different angles. That was one reason I wanted to talk to him. Also, because I knew he of all people would understand about racial prejudice.

But there was no chance for a careful discussion because Mum burst right in with "I'll see to this at the school tomorrow!"

"No!" I protested. "Don't you dare! I'm only telling you about it because Dad asked how my day was. I could use a little advice sometimes but the last thing I need is for you to go up there and make a scene!"

As I said this I gestured wildly and poked myself with the scissors. The back of my hand started to bleed. Making a run for the kitchen so I wouldn't drip on the sweatshirt, I rinsed the cut under the tap and started upstairs to look for a plaster.

Cass came in just then but she didn't speak to me. Her face looked a sickly pale under her thick make-up. I wanted to ask her if she and Paul had decided anything, but obviously this was the wrong time.

The box which held plasters was there but completely empty, so I folded a tissue into a small square and pasted it over the cut with cello tape. I definitely could not take any more craziness around here. But I had to face the possibility that we might be adding a baby with all its clutter and complication to the insane asylum that was our home.

THE PARK PACK

Walking to school through the park wasn't as bad as coming home that way. At least, not usually. The gang members all came to school from different directions and some didn't pass through the park at all. So it was pure bad luck if you ran into a pack of them, like I did the next morning.

It was one of those sunny mornings in September that make you forget we live on an island which spends most of the year being attacked by wet gale force winds. I wasn't late (okay, I admit, I'm never late) and I just sauntered along squinting my eyes, enjoying the feel of sun on my face.

When I opened my eyes next I noticed Ebony coming down the hill from the left side of the park, headed towards the gate nearest the school. I felt myself move into high gear so we wouldn't reach the gate at the same split second. I didn't want to have to think about whether to speak to her or not.

I speeded up until I was right behind a group of several kids. Then I noticed one of the girls had lacquered auburn hair so I hung back a bit. I didn't want to encounter queen bee Lou and her drones so soon after breakfast! Yesterday she nearly maims me for life, and here she is again like nothing happened. I could have ended up in a coma, and she probably just got told off, which wouldn't even make a dent in her attitude.

The gang were moving too slow for me so I started to walk around them. They were all nodding their heads in unison and clicking their fingers. It looked ridiculous and I would have laughed out loud if I wasn't such a wimp.

Just then some of them started chanting. They didn't even see me because they turned in unison to watch Ebony walking towards them. I stopped dead in my tracks, but not because of any desire to protect the black girl. From what I'd seen of her so far, she could take care of herself.

It was the lyrics I heard them singing that froze me. I stood still, trying to catch my breath and sort out in my mind what was happening. At first I just got snatches of it because they kept their voices low. But after a minute I was sure I'd heard correctly.

I never heard any song like that on the radio! As I listened a few more took it up the chant. "White is right, black is nil, the only solution is to kill kill kill!" They repeated it louder and louder as Ebony approached.

The black girl marched straight up to them, head held high. She looked ready to mow them down. With her long thin dark legs and high chunky heels she moved across the grass like an exotic bird. I saw her crumple a piece of paper she was holding and stuff it in her blazer pocket.

The closer she got, the louder they chanted, and by the time she was a few feet away the words were ringing sharply in the crisp air.

"White is right, black is nil, the only solution is to kill kill kill!"

It was like watching a film. I stood there mesmerized, waiting to see what would happen.

Ebony strode up to the gang like she was strolling alone on the planet Mars. They stood there chanting louder and louder, but she didn't slow down and her expression didn't change. She was a tough one! Her face was cool and uncaring, like there was nothing between her and the park exit but the ground she was walking on. Her dark eyes glittered faintly. It was like, she didn't admit their existence but if she had, it would have been so she could let them know she was better than they were.

They were all staring at her, daring her to flinch but she didn't. They had to jostle one another slightly to move aside as she cut a swath through their midst.

The gang paid no attention to me as I ran past them and walked quickly up the path heading to school to get ahead of Ebony. I didn't look back but as soon as the path bent sharply to the left I slowed down and glanced back. After a moment Ebony rounded the turn. She had taken the piece of paper out of her pocket and was reading it.

"Hello," I said.

Ebony gave a start and stuffed the paper back in her pocket, making a quick brushing motion across her eyes with the other hand. If it had been anyone else, I might have thought she was about to cry.

"You better tell me what your name is," she said, "'cause I keep on seeing you."

"It's Star."

"I'm Ebony." The muscles in her face relaxed some. She fell in step with me.

"I know," I said. "About that stuff back there—"

Ebony snorted loudly. "Honey, you ain't seen nothin'. That's just typical whitey crap." She glanced sideways at me and shrugged, as if she was sorry I had to be included in that deficient race.

We were nearly to the front doors of the school and I was about to ask Ebony if she wanted to sit with me at lunch.

Suddenly there was Adam at my side, looking drop-dead handsome with his hair falling over one eye.

"Hiya, Star," he said. "What lunch do you do– sandwiches or hot?"

"Hot." Like my face right now.

"Well, all my mates are off on a field trip today. You want to sit with me?" All of a sudden his face seemed to register who I was walking with.

I must have turned pale because he looked at me strangely. I swear I had completely forgotten my determination to avoid Ebony. That scene at the park, those awful words, had driven it completely out of my head.

"Y-uh, maybe so," I stammered.

"What you gonna do now, white girl?" whispered Ebony, then she scooted ahead of us up the steps into the school.

* * *

Well, I did sit with Adam at lunch. Of course he gave me another warning about my image. I nodded dutifully, watching his lips move and wondering what it would be like to kiss them. I've been kissed before, but I can't say it's happened all that often. Mostly it's been kind of like a science experiment: occasionally a guy will give you a snog just to see if he can figure out how it works, or maybe to add you to his collection.

I wanted to be more than that to Adam. I wanted us to be friends. And he was making it more and more clear that would mean giving Ebony the cold shoulder.

You'd think I would have spent a lot of time thinking about all this, trying to come to a sensible decision. I would have, too, except for what hit my eyes as I entered the art room that afternoon.

Our usual art teacher hadn't shown up this term. Rumour had it she'd been in a car crash and was still in hospital. So we'd had a couple of supply teachers who were about as artistic as Mr. Bean, and not nearly as funny. We'd all been hoping that our teacher would get well soon, because with our GCSE's coming up we didn't want to lose ground. Besides, we liked her and didn't want to think of her lying in hospital.

Well, the school had come up with a solution. They found a supply teacher who was extremely creative and artistic, and had just had something come up in her family which gave her a reason to want some extra cash.

I walked into the room completely unaware of all this. Perched on the teacher's stool, in all her turquoise splendour, sat my mum.

MY NAME, MY SHAME

I stopped so abruptly the person behind me scraped my heel. "Sorry," I muttered, moving out of the way. For a full minute I leaned hard against the door of the room, letting kids stream past me. Most didn't know who the new teacher was, and I took in their whispered comments.

"Check out the sweatshirt– did they find her at the circus?"

"I dunno– it's arty, anyway. Wonder if she made it herself?"

"She looks friendly."

"Yeah, she can't be worse than the last one."

Mum was smiling at them as they came in, but she managed to avoid looking at me. No wonder she was so quiet last night! I just stood there, wondering if I should leave. I felt like throwing up, so I could probably

spend the hour in the medical room. Or
maybe not. If you really were ill they called
your mother, and mine was too close for
comfort. Better stick it out. It was too late
to drop art as a GCSE and do something
else. Maybe I'd be lucky and she'd only
have us for a few days. I knew, though,
that Mum had trained as an art teacher but
had stopped teaching to have kids. She'd
probably even be good at it. But why oh why
did she have to be my mother?

"Hello, class," she began in an overly
cheery voice, "I'm Mrs. Smith. I'll be
teaching you while Miss Hooper is away.
You'll be glad to hear she is now out of
hospital, but it will be quite some time before
she's well enough to return. So I hope we'll
all get along." She smiled brightly, like a
nursery teacher with a class of half-wits.

I slunk into my seat. Out of the corners
of my eyes I glanced around the room and
couldn't believe what I was seeing. Most
of the kids seemed to be responding to her

friendliness instead of being turned off, the way I was. The only sullen face belonged to Matt and he didn't count because he always made trouble for supply teachers, just as a matter of principle. Anyway he wasn't any good at art; he just took it because he mistakenly thought it was an easy pass. I seemed to be stuck with him in most of my lessons– just my luck!

"I'll start with the register, so I can begin learning your names." Mum picked up the book and began to read the names aloud. I sat there under my own private black cloud, not paying much attention.

I should have been. If I'd been quicker off the mark, I could have foreseen and prevented what happened next.

"Jessica Read?"

"Yes, Miss."

"Emily Slater?"

"Yes, Miss."

"Andromeda Smith?"

For an instant the room was as quiet as

the universe before creation. The silence was followed by an outburst of puzzled questions, but then in unison every head swivelled in my direction.

"An-*drom*-e-da?" Matt repeated loudly. Everyone burst out laughing, although some of the girls sent me pitying glances.

I couldn't believe it. I had spent my whole school career making sure the teachers never used my first name. Even the most hardened teachers were sympathetic to my request.

So no one ever knew. Until now.

Through clenched teeth I said, "It's *Star*." I could feel my ears glowing red, pulsing like beacons on a lighthouse. Maybe an alien spaceship would land on the school roof and suck me up for experimental purposes. They could have me. I was ready to go.

"Oh yes, Star," Mum corrected. She went on calling out the other names as if her little slip was nothing important.

She'd probably forgotten her promise never ever to call me that in public. Maybe she never intended any harm. But the result was the same. My life was ruined.

Bad enough, that everyone in the whole school would know the truth by the end of today. Worse, I saw that people were starting to make the connection between Mum and myself. Might as well hang a poster around my neck, proclaiming in screaming metallic colours "I am Andromeda, daughter of the demented myth-loving sweatshirt-wearing Mrs. Smith!" I wished with all my might that she would just disappear.

I don't remember anything about the rest of the class. I'm sure we painted something. I think I threw my paper in the bin as I ran out of the class the moment the bell went.

One bad thing about school is, there's no private place you can go and cry your eyes out if you need to. I headed for the upper school cloakroom. Even though it's always crowded, there's a bench at the back on the other side of the lockers. The only spot in the school where you could sit without being seen.

I flung myself down on the bench and burst into tears, pulling my blazer lapels up to hide my face. Then my fogged brain registered that someone was already there, sitting next to me. I kept my head down and wiped my eyes with my fingers. There was a brown knee next to my white one.

"You too?" Ebony said.

I looked up and saw that the black girl's face was wet with tears. I couldn't believe it. What could possibly make *her* cry?

I nodded, digging in my blazer pocket for the packet of tissues I always carried. I offered Ebony one and she took it. I pulled out two and mopped up my own drips. I wanted to ask her what was wrong, but my attempts to be friendly with her tended to crash and burn.

"Having a bad day?" I asked finally.

"You said it, girl."

"Me too," I said. We sat there for a while, leaning our backs on the wall, staring at nothing. For some reason I felt a little better, just knowing someone else was miserable too. I was going to be very late for my next class and I didn't even care.

Suddenly Ebony thrust her hand into her pocket and dragged out a crushed piece of paper. She smoothed it out flat on her lap and stuck it in front of my face.

"Read this," she ordered.

I read it. It was a letter, written in blue ink on cheap lined paper with a strange kind of handwriting. I had to read it through a few times because some of it had got damp and the ink had run. Also, because the way of writing was odd.

Baby,

I got Leesha to write this down for me. She's in the bed next to mine in the infirmary. I can't write so good since I been sick. So she says she can write it for me but I'm telling her what to put down.

You don't need to worry none about me. They're pretty good to us here, being a prison. We get plenty to eat but sometimes

I don't feel like eating much so I give it to Leesha.

I ain't been a good mother to you Baby, and I'm real sorry about that. I prayed to the Lord to forgive me but I'm hoping your going to be able to forgive me too.

You say your real happy way over there in England with your daddy and his family. I'm real glad to hear that, so I won't have to worry about you. Anyhow I pray for you all the time, so I know the Lord is taking care of you.

Love, Momma

On my third read through the letter I began to grasp some of it. I couldn't just leave it there. We had to talk. Adam was going to have to accept that I would speak to Ebony occasionally.

"I'll walk you home today," I said.

Ebony gave a shrug and nodded.

HOMELESS IN MY HOME

We took the long way to Ebony's house. She walked in swift jerky movements. I had to stretch my legs to keep up.

By avoiding the park we were out of reach of the gang for now. A few people along the way stared at us, because like I said before there aren't many dark-skinned people around here.

I wanted to ask Ebony about the letter, but didn't know where to start. She did.

"My momma's in prison," she said, as casually as you'd say "It might rain today."

"Yeh, I figured that from the letter."

"There's something not right," she went on.

I thought she meant about being in prison, and I could agree with that. Although on days like today I wished my mother would be locked up somewhere!

"Last letter I got, she wrote herself. Said she had the flu. Now she says she can't find the strength to write the letter herself."

Ebony was quite a bit taller than me and I had to look up to see her face. Today her hair was braided in tiny plaits which bounced up and down like bouncing strings of licorice to the rhythm of her stride. I could see the worry in her dark eyes in spite of her usual stubborn expression.

"Who do you live with?" I asked.

"My daddy."

"So that family I saw you with at the badminton game–"

Ebony nodded. "That's my daddy and his wife and kids. He met my momma when he was in the States for a while."

"Then they got a divorce?"

"Naw. They never were married. He came back here and married Suzanne. Then when my momma got in trouble, he sent for me to come stay with them."

"And you like it here?"

Ebony blew out through her nose in a laugh that sounded more like a whinny. "You ignorant or somethin'?"

"Not especially. It's just she says that in the letter."

"Yeah, I tell her that. She's got enough to worry about without me tellin' her how much I hate this place."

Ebony didn't ask me to come in when we reached her house, but she smiled and waved when I said goodbye. There was a lot more I wanted to ask her, like how her mother ended up in prison and what all that "Lord" stuff in the letter meant, but it would keep. I had a feeling there'd be other times.

I felt a bit lightheaded as I trekked up the hill to my house. It had been so long since I'd had a friend. Maybe I could have a friendship with Ebony. At that point I was just enjoying the feeling that I might not be so alone any more, without thinking of any problems being her friend might cause.

I was still in a fog when I got home. Cass

was sitting on her bed which was strewn with leaflets. I grunted at her and went on through to my space.

Curled up bang in the middle of my cream-coloured duvet was a very guilty-looking black and white dog.

"Mopsy!" I shouted.

Mopsy slithered down and crept away, belly dragging the floor in apology.

"What's the idea, letting Mopsy on my bed?" I demanded, sticking my head back around to glare at Cass.

"Oh sorry, luv," she said, glancing up at me with a dreamy smile. I gritted my teeth over her "luv". We were back to Cass as usual, I guessed. "I didn't even notice she was in here. Look at this," she added, tossing one of the leaflets in my direction.

I picked it up off the floor, just as my mind began to register how you could actually see the floor for a change, and how Cass was wearing a white blouse trimmed with lace over her black skirt.

"Babies and benefits," I read aloud. "What's all this?"

Cass smiled again, and I noticed there was something different about her face. After a second I got it: she was still wearing make-up but it didn't look like she'd applied it with her normal Van Gogh technique.

I plopped down on the bed beside her and picked up another leaflet. "Pregnancy Related Illness," it said.

"Let me guess– you've seen the doctor."

"She had a cancellation so I got right in. She says I should have the baby. I'm strong and healthy and there's absolutely no reason not to."

"Have the baby! But that means–Cass, have you thought this through? If you have the baby, that means you'll have a baby! And then a toddler, and then a bratty little kid, and then a rebellious teen..." My imagination got going and I could even picture this monster child, a sort of horror version of Cass.

"Of course that's what it means!" she said, glaring at me. Then her face softened. "I'm not a complete idiot, no matter what you think. I know there'll be some big changes in my lifestyle."

"What about, you know, an abortion?"

"Yeah, well, it doesn't seem right to snuff out a life, even if it's not born yet."

I nodded. I figured that's how she'd feel and had to admit I agreed.

"Adoption?"

Cass gave me a scornful glance. "You read too many novels," she said.

After a minute she gave a shrug and continued. "Actually, the doctor tried to encourage me to think about that. She said there were lots of people who couldn't have children, who would give anything to have a baby. But I could never do that!"

"I don't see why not."

"Everybody would think I was a terrible person if I gave up my baby. I'd probably regret it the rest of my life!"

That didn't sound logical to me, but since when did Cass operate from logic?

"What about Paul?" I asked.

Cass sighed and her look turned to gloom. "I honestly don't know. We love each other, but I can't say we're ready to be married. I'm not even a hundred percent sure he's the one I want to marry."

I shrugged in sympathy and stared down at the bed, my eyes resting on a leaflet called "One Parent Benefit".

"Where..." I started, then stopped. I knew perfectly well that if Cass had a baby and still lived in this house, my little room would become a nursery. And we didn't have any other rooms available. I'd be homeless in my own home! I just didn't want to face talking about it right now.

As if she read my mind, Cass leaned forward and squeezed my arm.

"It'll work out, you'll see! It'll be a lot of fun, having a sweet little baby around the house."

The doorbell rang.

Cass jumped up. "Got to go... that's Paul. See you later!" She ran over to the dresser and gave herself a quick squirt of strong perfume, glanced in the mirror and fluffed her hair (back to blonde today), grinned at me like life was a bowl of cherries, and then was gone.

Oh sure, having a baby around would be a barrel of laughs. Screams at three a.m., stinky nappies, puke stains on your clothes. And where would I sleep? Out in the garage next to the washer?

An idea came to me. Mrs. Hinkeldorf lived in a house the same size as ours, all by herself. Maybe she would rent me a room. Peace and quiet and a room all to myself.

What on earth was I thinking? I liked things neat and clean but I was a slob compared to Mrs. H. I bet she'd do regular inspections of my underwear drawer. She'd have me clipping her lawn with nail scissors; she'd roust me out early on a Sunday and drag me to church– I shook my head until I was dizzy, to clear it of this bizarre scenario.

I wondered what Ebony would have to say about Cass's problem. After all, she herself had been a baby like that, born to a single mum. Would she say her mum did the right thing, having her and not giving her up for adoption? I thought I might ask her, next time I saw her.

* * *

That time came sooner than I expected, since both of us had detention the next day for being late when we were blubbering behind the lockers.

The assistant Head, Mrs. Frost, glared at us when we walked through the door of her office after school. Her pointy face looked like the edge of an axe as she lectured us on the virtues of punctuality and told us to go pick up all the litter in the schoolyard. I mentally switched off and occupied my mind with creating cartoon caricatures of her.

"Do you understand?" She demanded.

"Yes, Miss," I mumbled.

"Yes, Ma'am," Ebony said cheerily.

"And don't call me Ma'am!" Mrs. Frost snapped.

She handed us two plastic bags and we went outside. I was so humiliated I'm sure my face looked like a ripe tomato. I had never had detention for anything, and certainly not for being late! A drizzle was falling. I hunched my shoulders against the damp as I picked up soggy wads of paper.

Ebony on the other hand seemed chuffed. She even hummed a little tune under her breath as she bent down to scoop up crisp packets and sweet wrappers.

"Why are you so happy?" I grumbled.

"I'm glad I got punished. This school is so damn nice, they're trying so hard to help me fit in, but I don't want to." She wiped the rain off her face with one hand and gave me a little smile. She had nice hands, I noticed, slender with incredibly long but well-kept nails.

"Why not?"

"I want to get out of here! I'm gonna keep on pushing until they kick me right out, then my Daddy'll see he needs to send me back home to Texas."

"But you don't have a home there, do you?" I blurted out. "I mean, with your mum in prison." I was sorry the minute I'd said it.

Ebony's face hardened but there was something else in her eyes, maybe fear.

"She'll get parole some time. They let you out early if you're good. Then we can live together and I'll take care of her."

Somehow I guessed that told me the answer to the question I'd been planning to ask, and I didn't bring it up. Maybe Cass was doing the right thing after all. I felt like someone had punched me in the stomach and for a minute I couldn't think why. But then I realised it was because I'd thought I was making a friend, only to find she couldn't wait to leave.

Maybe that feeling was also some kind of premonition, my emotions forecasting future events.

LEVEL ONE – IT BEGINS

It started bright and early the next day. The persecution. That's how I always think of it, though it was nothing as bad as what Jews, Christians, blacks or whoever have gone through. But it felt like persecution to me and gave me a glimpse of what that might be like, to be shunned and mistreated for something you couldn't help, like the colour of your skin or the family you came from.

The first hint I had was only a whisper.

"Because she's her *mum*, that's why!"

The two girls in front of me glanced back then looked away when they saw I noticed. They giggled and began to jog, then started chatting again when they were well ahead, too far away for me to hear. I could hear their laughter though, echoing back to me past groups of pupils heading for the school. I was almost the only person walking alone.

I can't help it that she's my mum and I can't help having a weird name! I wanted to yell at the top of my lungs.

I trudged into the building in a foul mood, not realising that this was nothing to what was ahead.

It soon became clear to me that the gang was more clever than I thought. They obviously had spies everywhere, because they knew I had walked home with Ebony two days before, and as the saying goes, they were not amused.

"Level One" was what we called it at our school, the initial stage of treatment for the gang's displeasure. I say the gang but I knew it was all run by Lou and Matt. The rest were just wannabes who'd follow anyone strong enough to lead them.

As soon as I dropped off my coat and headed for the form room, I got a Level One. Our school has narrow corridors and trying to cram hundreds of kids into them during the few minutes between classes is a health hazard at the best of times. At worst, you get shoved on purpose and nobody can ever prove it was deliberate.

So I got shoved, slammed into the wall quickly and systematically. It knocked the wind out of me and I banged my nose hard. I didn't even see who did it. I didn't need to. It had all the earmarks of a gang-ordered incident. I was swept along by the tide of kids trying to catch my breath, random thoughts like "I'm seeing stars" and "No, I *am* Star," rocketing around in my head. My eyes were watering from the pain in my nose.

"Are you okay, Star?" It was Adam, looking concerned.

"Oh, yeh, well not really." My eyes leaked even more at his sympathy.

"Got a Level One, didn't you." He put his hand on my shoulder and gave a little squeeze.

I nodded. "Do you think my nose is broken?" I touched it gingerly and the throbbing pain shot up a notch.

Adam bent down to get a better look and our foreheads touched lightly. All of a sudden I didn't notice the pain so much.

"I don't think so, but maybe you should go put some ice on it." He sighed and shook his head.

"They're a right bunch of berks," he added, "but you know you only brought it on yourself. I tried to warn you."

He had warned me, and I'd agreed with what he said but then done the opposite. I couldn't sort out my thoughts at that moment to explain why I hadn't followed his advice.

Even in my dizzy state I was aware this was only the beginning of problems with the gang. That's the way they operated: start small and work up. Level One, a shove. Level Two, you took a few hard kicks in the shins; Level Three, your P.E. things went missing. Level Four was a beating, and at Level Five you could count on landing in casualty. I only know of one boy who got a Level Five, and we never saw him again.

Usually it didn't take more than a Level Three for the gang to manipulate you into doing whatever it was they wanted.

"Meet me for lunch again?" he asked.

I gave him a grateful smile and accepted. That would give me some time to think it over, come up with some explanation to satisfy him, as to why I was spending time with Ebony. My heart was responding to him again, and I practically floated into the form room. Maybe I could make him see that I didn't want to reject Ebony just because she was black. Then it would be all right between us again. Maybe he'd even ask me to go out with him.

My first lesson of the day was history. Right away I noticed Ebony had painted her fingernails. Other people were looking at them too. Even Lou sitting behind her tried to glance over Ebony's shoulder when she thought no one saw her.

I'd never seen fingernail art before, except in magazines or on the telly. Ebony had painted a picture in bright colours on each nail. I couldn't tell what they were without moving closer. Ebony was asking for trouble, coming to school with her nails decorated.

Then it hit me. That's why she did it. She was trying to get in trouble; she'd told me so herself. This was a move in her campaign to get kicked out and sent back to Texas. I wondered what else she had planned. She was going to keep on pushing the limits until the school would say they'd had enough.

The thought was discouraging. It occurred to me there wasn't much point in keeping on trying to be friends with Ebony. I could back out now and save myself some hassle, since she'd be leaving anyway. Maybe she wouldn't care. Maybe inside that hard shell there weren't any feelings– although I knew that wasn't true, because I'd seen her cry.

But I really didn't want to give up Adam. If I told him she was planning to leave, that might take the pressure off. Then I could somehow juggle them both until Ebony went.

By this time Miss Wellbeck had become aware no one was listening to her, since we were all staring at Ebony's fingernails. She marched down the aisle and stopped by Ebony's desk. Ebony sat straight and spread out her hands for viewing. She looked up coldly, a challenge in her eyes.

"Ebony," said Miss Wellbeck sternly, wrinkling her pudgy features into a frown, "you know that's not allowed!"

We were all wondering if she'd send Ebony right down to the science lab to remove the art. She hesitated, then took the easy option. "Make sure that's off by tomorrow."

There was a slight sigh of relief from the girls in the class, because we were all dying to see the paintings up close before they were destroyed.

After the lesson all the girls except Lou crowded around Ebony in the corridor. On one thumbnail a fierce tiger glared from a background of jungle foliage. The other thumbnail was an American flag. Every single nail was different, each done in painstaking detail.

"Why aren't you doing GCSE art?" one of the girls asked.

Ebony shrugged. She held out her hands so we could see them but didn't make any attempt to be friendly.

"I can't believe you'll have to remove it," another said.

"Yeh, why don't you keep it on? That must have taken hours!"

"Naw, not that long," Ebony replied. "I do this stuff all the time, so I'm real fast."

"By the way," the first girl said, "do you know about the concert?" She reached in her pocket and pulled out some orange cards.

We each took one, and I saw the words "Big City" in bold letters, with some details underneath.

"Never heard of them," someone said.

"Oh, they're really good. The concert's in a fortnight, right here in the school hall."

Two of the other girls who I recognized as gang wannabes rolled their eyes behind the first girl's back. Then they hurried away, whispering. I wondered what that was all about but I just stuffed the card into a pocket and didn't give it another thought until later.

"We'd better run or we'll be late," I said. At that everyone scurried off to their next lesson, calling out thank-you's to Ebony.

She walked with me down the corridor. I thought she should be pleased that everyone was so friendly, but she didn't say anything.

"That was cool," I said finally.

Ebony wrinkled her forehead at me like she felt sorry I was so retarded.

"You don't get it," she said.

"Don't get what?"

"Shoot, girl, they don't care about me! I clean my nails, I go right back to being just a big black girl they don't want to have nothin' to do with."

"But I'm not like that!" I protested.

Ebony glanced sideways at me as we pushed through the blue-blazered mob.

"Maybe you're not. Or maybe you're not as good as you think you are. That boyfriend of yours'll tell you to keep out of my way, and what you gonna do? Which way you gonna jump, white girl?"

She turned abruptly and headed for the door to the other building, leaving me standing there, watching her bushy hair bounce up and down above the crowd.

I was furious. Who did she think she was, the Queen of Sheba? She was so arrogant! She was so– I didn't know what! Or maybe I did. Maybe she was right.

As I walked to my next lesson I began to calm down and think it over. Did I really want to be Ebony's friend, or did I just want a friend for myself, because no one else would have me? Was I willing to put any future relationship with Adam on the line for her sake?

She'd asked the right question. Which way would I jump? Both, if I could. But that might not be possible.

Behind me there was some kind of commotion going on outside the door of the assistant Head's study. Several voices were raised and my heart dropped to my school shoes because they sounded extremely familiar.

THIS STAR NEEDS SOME SPARKLE

"But, Mum!" wailed a small red-haired boy. "They won't get away, I promise! I'll keep them in my pocket."

Perse and Jase stood side by side, looking like hobbits in their huge blazers. Whatever this was about they'd be in it together.

Mum wore an egg-yellow sweatshirt, dotted with sequins. She shook her head firmly and held out a cardboard box.

"Put them in here right now," she said. "I'll set them out in the car."

"They'll suffocate and die!" Jase wailed.

"Right now!" Mum's voice boomed out. Lots of heads turned.

Mrs. Frost stood with arms folded at the door of her study. I couldn't tell if she was more annoyed with the boys for whatever they'd done or at Mum for having such awful kids.

Reluctantly both boys reached into their blazer pockets and dug out several small squirming bodies. Baby guinea pigs might be sweet but I could just picture them escaping...having more baby guinea pigs... the school overrun with furry creatures...I couldn't help smiling, but my smile froze as Mum stalked over to Mrs. Frost, clutching her carton of guinea pigs.

"I have to say, Mrs. Frost, this seems a tempest in a teapot to me."

Mrs. Frost straightened her spine, which took some doing since it was already stiff as steel. She glared at Mum through her thick glasses.

"Mrs. Smith, surely you realise that we cannot have animals running loose in the school."

"Of course not, Mrs. Frost," Mum replied, in a tone that said she was about to donate a piece of her mind. "However, I think your energies might be better directed at discovering what really goes on in those drama lessons. My daughter was nearly injured seriously the other day–"

At that I turned and ran before Mum could see me and yell "Andromeda"! I couldn't believe it– after I had especially asked her not to say anything. She just couldn't be trusted! I wished Dad would keep her locked up at home but I'd never seen him try to influence her in anything. She did or said whatever she wanted, and he just went along with it.

I stalked furiously to my next class, scattering year seven kids right and left. Life wasn't fair! Out of all the parents in the world, I had to be stuck with *my* mum and dad!

Surprisingly I found I was more angry at Dad. Maybe if he took charge things would be different in our family! Maybe Cass wouldn't be in such a fix. Maybe I'd be able to invite people home because it wouldn't be a tip!

This was a new thought because for years I'd blamed Mum for the way things were. It's unnerving to think one way about something for a long time and then in a flash see it the opposite.

Over lunch I tried to explain about Ebony to Adam– how she was just acting up to get expelled, and then she would get expelled so she wouldn't be a problem anymore, and how I would feel really low just ignoring her.

He nodded and looked deep into my eyes with his dark blue ones, making me lose my appetite completely even though there was a plate of hot chips waiting to be devoured. I was painfully aware of how tatty my hair was and decided right then I'd see if Cass could do something with it after school.

"You see," I explained to Adam, "she's actually a very nice person, once you get to know her."

His forehead wrinkled. I don't think he got what I meant.

"I just hate to see you lower yourself," he said. "I think more of you than that."

I felt an indescribable mix of emotions wash over me, like taking ten completely different colours and swirling them together. Part of me was saying, he thinks a lot of me! Maybe he'll even ask me to go out with him!

Part of me felt wounded, like someone had insulted me, only I wasn't sure why.

And another part was saying, which way you gonna jump, white girl?

* * *

So I jumped to the hairdressers that afternoon, instead of going home. Muddled didn't half describe the state of my brain, so I thought I'd just try decorating the outside of it instead of worrying about the mass of conflicting thoughts on the inside.

Cass was standing over an old lady when I walked through the salon door, winding her fluffy white hair onto tiny perm rollers. When I told her what I wanted, she said, "No problem– just have a seat. Mrs. Brown is my last customer."

I sat and thumbed through a hairstyle magazine, inhaling toxic chemicals while trying to pick a style. There didn't seem to be any that were even in the general range of normal. I gave it up and just hoped Cass could be trusted not to go too dramatic.

A couple of hours later I was gazing in the mirror at the new Star Smith.

"Do you like it?" Cass asked anxiously.

I just stared. It was different. She'd kept it just above shoulder length, but now I had a feathery fringe which blended in with layers falling softly around my face. The basic shade was the same dull brownish-blonde, but there were streaks a few tints lighter. If you didn't know, you might have thought it was all my natural colour. It just gave my hair a bit of sparkle.

I grinned up at Cass in the mirror and she let her shoulders drop with a sigh of relief.

"I love it!" I said. "I really really do."

"I'll pay for it," she said with a big grin as she whisked away the purple cape I was wearing.

"But I'll pay you back at home. You know me, I've always got money saved up."

Cass laughed at that; my stinginess was a legend in our family. I stood up and we gave each other a quick hug.

* * *

I was disappointed the next day was Saturday. That meant I'd have to wait until Monday to see if Adam reacted to the new me.

That morning instead of quickly running a comb through my hair I spent half an hour in front of the mirror in my room, carefully combing it until I thought it looked almost as good as when Cass had done it the day before. She'd left early to work at the salon.

As I styled my hair I thought about how different things were now between Cass and me. I guess it started with the baby, so at least some good had come out of it. I had never ever thought of Cass as a potential friend, but now I could see it might happen.

I put on some eye make-up and decided I looked a hundred percent better than usual, then wondered who would even notice or care.

What about Ebony? True, we hadn't exactly parted on good terms and I still wasn't sure how I'd answer her question. I didn't have it all sorted out in my mind but I found myself heading out the door in the direction of her house.

On the way I couldn't help looking behind me a few times to see if anyone from school saw me. During school hours I couldn't shake the prickly feeling between my shoulderblades which told me there were kids watching me, ready to punish me if I got too friendly with Ebony.

"Lookin' good!" was the first thing Ebony said when she opened the door. She gave a big grin. "I like it." I was happy I hadn't even had to tell her something was different.

"Thanks. I just thought I'd come by and see if you'd notice I had it done." I was about to leave but she motioned me inside.

"Come on in. Everybody else went to the pool, but I wasn't in the mood."

BLAME IT ON CHINESE TAKEAWAYS

I couldn't help staring around as we went inside and up the stairs. It was just an ordinary house, not much different than ours except with less clutter. Even her room wasn't anything unusual, although most of the posters on the wall were of black music groups or actors.

There was one big difference though.

"That is totally amazing," I said when I saw her desk.

It was nearly covered with tiered black plastic shelves holding dozens of bottles of nail varnish, every colour imaginable. There was a tray of special fine-tipped brushes, a plastic cube full of cotton wool and a giant bottle of varnish remover. A small blue towel was laid out at the front of the white desk top.

"You want a manicure?" she asked. I

noticed she had removed the fingernail art and her nails were painted a metallic green.

"Sure– but my nails are really a mess." I held out the chewed and mangled specimens for her to see.

"Doesn't matter."

Ebony motioned for me to sit on the stool and left the room for a second, coming back with a metal folding chair for herself.

"I can paint you a picture, anything you want." She seemed more at ease than I'd ever seen her. That made me realise how much of a protective shell she normally wore.

I shook my head. "Just a plain colour. I don't have your kind of nerve."

Ebony smiled and gave a shrug. "You'd been through what I have, you would."

I watched silently while she rubbed my cuticles with softening cream. Then I asked, "You mean about your mum?"

Her eyes clouded over. "Naw. That's real bad, but I just mean the plain old stuff people lay on you because you're black.

That's what you'll never have to put up with."

I wasn't so sure. If people knew the full truth about the Smiths, I might get the same kind of treatment. Maybe someday I'd tell Ebony a bit more about our family.

When the manicure was complete I sat with both elbows on the desk and hands in the air to let my newly polished nails dry. I'd picked a light pink shade; brighter colours were tempting but I wasn't willing to get in trouble at school over my nails. She'd done a great job; you'd never have guessed how much time I spent biting them. I resolved to turn over a new leaf.

While we waited for the nails to dry Ebony began to pace back and forth across the room. She seemed to forget I was there; I had the feeling she was somewhere else entirely, seeing something she didn't like.

"What's wrong?" I asked finally, after about the twentieth time she'd crossed the room.

She stopped and stared at me, then gave a big sigh and flopped down in the folding chair. She pulled her legs up and hugged her knees, staring down at her gold house slippers.

"I'm worried about my momma," she said, resting her chin on her knees. "There's lots of people who deserve to be locked up, but not her! Why does she have to go through this?" she demanded like it was my fault, but I knew she was just upset.

"They put her inside 'cause she stabbed her lover, but he was nothin' but low-down trash. He beat her up and tried to kill her, so of course she's gonna stab him in self-defence! Didn't even kill him, he's walking around enjoying his sorry life. She couldn't afford a hotshot lawyer so there she is, stuck behind bars like she's some animal in a zoo."

I remembered something from her mother's letter which puzzled me, so I brought it up to try and distract her. "What do you think she means, when she talks about 'the Lord'?".

She ignored me. "I gotta go see her, but my daddy says I have to wait till summer. Summer! She needs me now."

"Why don't you go in the autumn break, or at Christmas?"

Ebony shook her head. "It's the money. You wouldn't believe how much a ticket costs. He says he's got to save up some."

I couldn't see any answer to that– even if Ebony got a part-time job, it would take a long time to save for a plane ticket.

"About this 'Lord' stuff," she added, "I don't exactly understand it myself. I asked her about it last time I wrote. I know for sure Momma's different, though. She's always been a real nice person and all, but now she's got some kind of peace she never had."

Ebony stopped staring at her feet and looked up at me. "Sometimes I wish I could get that kind of peace," she said in a low intense voice. "Living in this poor excuse for a country– 'scuse me for saying it in front of you– having to see my daddy act like the perfect family man, when all the time my momma's hurtin'....Chinese takeaways!"

"Chinese takeaways?" I asked, confused.

"Yeah, we got to eat that junk about every other day, seems like. I hate it here!

"Oh, forget it," she said abruptly. "Let's go see a movie."

So we did. Caught the bus to the cinema and saw the latest film, the one everyone at school had been raving about. It was a lot of fun, too. Ebony seemed to have switched off the part of her where she thought about her mother and hating England. I guess she had a kind of cupboard inside her where she could lock everything up when she needed to.

On the way home on the bus we laughed and talked about the film as if we'd known each other for ages. I couldn't remember when I'd had such a good time.

The bus wheezed and squeaked as it slowed down for the next stop.

The smile wiped from Ebony's face as if it

had never been there.

"What is it?"

"Here comes trouble," she said.

Matt climbed aboard the bus and showed the driver his pass. Two older guys were with him, real skinheads by the look of them. One of them wore a T-shirt, even though it was jacket weather. They didn't have passes and tossed coins into the driver's pay slot.

Matt grinned when he saw us and the three took a seat a couple of rows behind ours. As they passed our seat, I noticed the skinhead with the T-shirt had a spider web tattooed on his upper arm.

I felt Ebony go stiff. I glanced at her and gave a start. That was the first time that day I'd thought of her particularly as being black, as in "Here I am being friends with a black girl." She was just a person I was getting to know and like. But Matt's arrival changed that– I still liked her just as much but I suddenly became very aware of her skin colour.

I sat back with my cheeks burning. It

made me furious that a couple of slap-heads could have that kind of power over me!

Ebony pretended she didn't see Matt. Her face took on that stony look she normally wore and the rest of our time was ruined. We just sat there quietly like two people who happened by coincidence to be sharing the same seat on a bus.

* * *

No surprises in the school corridor on Monday when I got a "Level Two", a few hard kicks on the ankles which left me gasping in pain.

"Walk home with me," I barked at Ebony when I passed her. I wasn't even asking; it was an order.

"Did you get a Level Two today?" I asked her as we left the school gates.

"A what?" she asked, so I explained. She shook her head. That was interesting.

"Why don't we go to my house," I said. I was really living dangerously today!

I waved at Mrs. Hinkeldorf who was

staring out her window when Ebony and I
walked up the drive. She didn't wave back,
and her eyes were bulging out of her head.

"Your neighbour always look like that?"
Ebony asked.

"No."

We looked at one another and giggled.
I guess that was the first time we began to
treat the whole black-white thing like some
big joke.

Ebony didn't seem at all bothered by the
clutter inside, but she did jump back when
Mopsy charged through the kitchen door.

"Mops!" I yelled, grabbing her just in
time before Ebony's school tights became
rags.

Baldy came out of the lounge to see what
was happening and he gave Ebony a big
smile like he thought it was totally normal
for me to have a friend over. What a kid!
I ruffled his curly hair and motioned for
Ebony to follow me up the stairs.

As we passed through Cass's part of the

room, I reminded myself to thank Cass for starting to keep her area a bit neater. It wasn't perfect but at least you could walk without having to kick aside discarded clothes.

"This is my room," I said, flinging back the sunflower curtain.

Ebony stepped past the curtain. With two of us in there it was crowded so I hopped onto the bed. Ebony moved around the tiny space with her fidgety movements, occasionally touching a knick-knack. This made me nervous and I held my breath, hoping she wouldn't break anything. I didn't want to turn into a Mrs. Hinkeldorf but I wasn't used to inviting anyone into my private world.

She picked up Adam's photo and looked at it for a second, then glanced at me with a question in her eyes. I knew what that question was. Which way would I jump? So far my answer was "both ways" but I didn't feel like trying to explain that right now. I didn't think she'd understand, and I couldn't really blame her.

She set the photo back down and joined me on the bed. We were just in the middle of a good chat about music when the doorbell rang and Mopsy started barking. I listened for any sounds that the boys were responding, but all was quiet except for Mopsy.

I sighed. "I have to do everything around here!" I complained, as Ebony followed me back downstairs.

She was right behind me when I opened the door to Mrs. Hinkeldorf, who was holding out an empty teacup.

"Star," Mrs. H. began. I noticed she managed to get my name right today. "I do not have enough sugar to finish my cake. May I please borrow a cup of sugar?"

A REASON TO START HATING

"Of course, Mrs. Hinkeldorf," I said in my most welcoming voice, taking the teacup from her. "Come in and meet my friend."

Ebony and I traded amused glances over Mrs. H.'s head as she stepped into the hall, after looking carefully at the floor. She must have thought we kept the boa constrictor loose in the house.

"Mrs. Hinkeldorf, this is Ebony," I said.

"Pleased to meet you, ma'am," Ebony said, sticking out her hand.

Mrs. H. stared up at Ebony, her beady eyes registering amazement. She was so short she had to crane her neck back to see Ebony's face and her tight grey curls quivered. She managed to spit out something that might have been "Likewise" but she didn't offer her hand. Probably it was because she was so busy trying to work out where Ebony's accent was from; at least, I'd give her the benefit of the doubt on that.

I took her cup through to the kitchen and poured it full of sugar. When I came back into the hall, Mrs. H. and Ebony were just standing there silently, each staring at a different part of the wallpaper.

Mrs. H. took the cup, thanked me, and gave Ebony one long stare up and down before she left.

* * *

On Tuesday at school we both got a Level Three. I'd been expecting that, but not the other thing that happened.

I was in a hurry for P.E. so I raced from French lesson to the cloakroom, grabbed my kit and ran for the gym. I didn't even notice that the rucksack seemed a lot lighter than usual. It wasn't until I dumped everything out in the changing room that I realised my trainers and sweatshirt were missing.

"Somebody took my trainers," I complained to Miss Cleeves.

"Don't be silly, Star," she snapped, because she was trying to deal with five girls who said they had their period and couldn't play hockey. Four of the five seemed to have a period about every other week, and I guess she was tired of the scam. I turned my back on her in a sulk. She knew I wasn't the type to forget my things!

There was no doubt in my mind this was planned by the gang. I went to look for Ebony. She was just coming to find Miss Cleeves, P.E. rucksack in hand and steam coming out of her ears.

"You too?" I asked, and she nodded. The beads on her plaits clicked furiously.

"I got those shoes in the States and there's no way I could afford that brand over here. You tell me who it was, and I swear I'm gonna knock some heads together!"

"I don't know who. I just know it was the gang– but that means Matt and Lou made it happen." I grinned as I had a mental picture of Ebony, who was taller than both Matt and

Lou, grabbing them by the scruff of the neck and cracking their foreheads together.

The surprising thing was what happened next.

"Star," called one of the girls with her period– the only one who seemed genuine– "you can use my trainers. We're about the same size." We had art together and I knew her name was Amy but I'd never talked with her particularly.

Amy rummaged in her rucksack and pulled out her trainers, tossing them at me.

The other four girls who weren't doing P.E. sat there for a minute. Then one of them looked at Ebony's feet.

"Mine might fit you," she said.

They loaned us their sweatshirts as well, so both Ebony and I were kitted out and able to join the others on the hockey pitch. The weather had turned cool and rainy, but I was glad we were able to play.

Miss Cleeves smiled and nodded when she saw us, so it looked like we wouldn't be in her black books. She was a good teacher but the kind you needed to stay on the right side of. Once she got a poor opinion of you, she tended to keep it forever no matter what you did.

Our P.E. stuff magically appeared in our rucksacks before the end of school. Must have been because the trick didn't work, with the other girls loaning us theirs. It probably seemed safer to whoever did the deed to return the things and not be caught with them.

I looked for Amy during lunch break and finally found her huddled with a group of girls, trying to protect themselves from the chilly drizzle because we were absolutely not allowed back inside the building until the bell went, unless it was pouring. They don't care if we get pneumonia or not, rules are rules.

"Amy, thanks for that," I said. I'd already told her twice but I was extremely grateful.

"I like your hair, Star," one of the other girls said.

Amy smiled at me in a friendly way. She had short blonde hair and pleasant features. "Yeh, it's nothing. By the way, don't forget about the concert."

"What concert?"

"You know, I gave you a card about it last week."

Oh right, I remembered. I stuck my hand in my blazer pocket and pulled out the orange piece of paper.

"Big City," I read aloud. "What kind of a group is that?"

For a minute Amy seemed flustered. "They're– uh, it's kind of hard to describe, but really good. Really up, you know?"

I didn't know, but I thanked her again and turned to leave.

"Oh, and be sure and invite your friend," she called after me.

My friend. Oh great, now the whole school had me pegged as Ebony's friend. Well, she was. There, I'd admitted it to myself!

But I'd still had my absurd little fantasy

of keeping the friendship secret. No chance of that, I realised, with someone as visible as Ebony.

Okay, so there goes that. But maybe Adam would change his mind. People did change all the time. Just when you thought you really knew someone, they'd do something completely out of character. Probably he felt the way he did about blacks because his parents taught him that. Maybe I could teach him differently. I'd at least make it my mission in life to try!

Come to think of it, he'd have to change if he was going to get to know me. Because once he found out the truth about the Smith family....

With the cat out of the bag regarding Ebony I decided to walk home with her. What she decided was to go straight through the park. A bad choice, I said, but she had her reasons.

"See, it's like this," she explained as we left school. "You gotta fight hate with hate.

They hate me, so I hate them back more. And I let them see it. I don't get into a fight with them 'cause I'd lose that for sure, but they need to see my hate. That way, I win."

I mulled that one over as we walked along.

"I don't think I'm a very good hater," I said finally.

"Naw, you're too nice. But you don't have as much reason to hate as me. You don't have much practice."

"How do you know I don't have a reason? Maybe you don't know everything about me."

Ebony laughed harshly. "Honey, whatever you're talkin' about, you're clueless as to what it's like to look like me in a place like this."

Maybe she it was true that she needed hate as a weapon of defense. But the only reason I didn't need it was because my dad had chosen to hide the truth about our family. Which way was better, hiding or

hating? Couldn't there be a middle ground
somewhere?

I thought the bad weather would keep
the gang from clogging the park entrance,
but there they were as usual. They looked
like a swarm of orange bees with their black
bomber jackets turned inside out so the
orange lining showed. At the core were Lou
and Matt, lighting fags– probably spliffs,
from the way they were holding them. It's
hard to get a joint lit and look cool passing
it around with the wind dumping cold rain
down the back of your neck, but they were
sure trying.

Ebony didn't even slow down, she just
headed right for the middle, wearing her
most arrogant look. I hurried to keep up
with her, my heart pounding.

For once they didn't try to block her
path. Matt moved to one side and Lou to
the other, and their groupies did the same.
Ebony and I sauntered down the middle.
She didn't make eye contact with anyone but

waves of hatred poured out of her. I tried to imitate her disdainful glare but figured I just looked like my lunch disagreed with me.

"Nigger-lover!" The words hissed into my ear like venom from a snake just as I passed by Lou. I couldn't help twisting my head to look at her. Her auburn hair tossed in the wind and her eyes glimmered with loathing.

I jerked my head back and stared into the distance until we were well past the group. The force of her malice was like a physical thing, punching me in the stomach. My insides felt like they were crumbling into tiny jagged pieces. What had I ever done to her? Maybe according to the gang, a white who hung around with blacks was even worse than blacks themselves.

"What do you think, girl?" Ebony said when we were well out of their hearing. "Maybe now you better start learnin' to hate."

OUT WITH THE FAMILY SECRET

I couldn't deny it really shook me when Lou spit those words at me. I found myself turning right instead of left after Ebony and I said goodbye, heading for town and the hairdressers. Last time I tried to go to Cass with a problem, she'd told me she was pregnant. But now, the way we were getting along better and all, I decided to try again. I needed to talk with someone who wasn't so close to the trouble.

"Hiya, little sis," Cass greeted me cheerily.

The salon wasn't busy and Cass sat at the reception desk, filing her nails.

"Hi," I said. "And don't call me 'little sis'– it's embarrassing."

"Sure, whatever."

"Cass–" I began, about to launch into the details of what had just happened in the park.

"It's all decided," she cut in, not even hearing me.

"What is?"

"About the– you know." She lowered her voice. I guessed she hadn't said anything to the salon owner about her condition.

"I'm going to keep the baby and live at home. Paul and I just aren't sure about our future, and his parents keep saying 'Two wrongs don't make a right.' Maybe we'll get married later on, but it just isn't right for now. We can make your part of the room into the nursery."

Cass smiled up at me, her plump cheeks rosy and free of make-up. She had on her white blouse again, and tiny gold studs in her ears instead of giant hoops.

I stood in front of the desk, stunned into silence. Nobody consulted me about this! Did she just assume it would be perfectly okay to take over my one private space?

And she could have been more aware that I was about to unload a problem on her. So much for becoming friends with my sister!

I didn't trust myself to speak. I stormed out of the salon, not even glancing back to see if she looked puzzled or hurt.

When I reached the house there was a piece of paper sticking out of the letter slot. My mind was still churning and I unfolded it automatically because my name was printed on the outside. I hardly saw the words at first.

Then I dropped my school bags, kicked off my shoes and raced up to my room. I sank down on the bed and spread out the piece of paper. There was no mistake. Below the sign of a swastika someone had printed in pencil,

WHITEY, BE WARNED.

STICK WITH YOUR OWN KIND. CHANGE YOUR WAYS AND YOU CAN CHANGE THE FUTURE.

There was no signature, but it didn't need one. I was right– for some reason, white people who were friendly with people who weren't their "own kind" made creeps like Matt and Lou go spare.

I ran downstairs and rang Ebony's number, which she'd given me on Saturday.

"I just got a note through the door," I said when she answered.

"Me too."

"I'm coming over."

At Ebony's house we sat on the floor of her room on a bright-coloured rug and showed each other the letters. Hers also bore a crude swastika and said simply

WHITE IS RIGHT, BLACK IS NIL, THE ONLY SOLUTION IS TO KILL, KILL, KILL.

"Same old boring stuff," she said with a shrug.

"Maybe this is connected with neo-Nazis– like those skinheads we saw on the bus. My dad showed me an article in the paper– they're trying to stir up trouble around here."

"Yeah, I bet you're right. You know what that spider web tattoo means? You get to wear that if you've killed a black person."

My insides seized up like they'd been fast-frozen. No wonder Ebony went all stiff when she saw them! "What do you think they'll do?" My voice was going squeaky.

"Whatever they think they can get away with. Beat us up real bad, stick a knife in us." She might have been saying they'd offer us a mint. She gazed at the swirling pattern on the rug, picking at a loose thread with her fingers. Her nails were painted in metallic swirls, like she'd copied the rug.

"I don't think they'd use knives," I said. "There are all these strict laws here now, and the police can search you if they think you might have one."

"You're kiddin' me, girl! Where I come from, you can carry a gun, as long as you got a permit." Ebony sighed and hesitated.

"I really dropped you in it, didn't I," she went on. "You don't have to stick around. You better get out while the gettin's good."

I shook my head firmly. "No way. All for one and one for all."

"Huh?"

"Never mind– just something I read in a book once. Okay, I admit I'm scared to death, but I can't just turn my back on you."

Ebony frowned. "You got some idea of this bein' your duty, to be nice to blacks?"

I thought about that and it made me squirm. How much of my wanting to befriend Ebony was due to a streak of the do-gooder in me?

"Maybe that's partly true," I admitted, and Ebony tossed her head to show her disapproval.

"But it's more than that." I took a deep breath. "I don't have friends, really, and I thought that the two of us could be friends."

She stared at me for a second. Then she smiled. "That's cool."

"Show you something else," she added, reaching up to pull a piece of paper from her desk. I could see right away it was another letter from her mother. It was on the same cheap lined paper in the same handwriting as the first one. She laid it out on the rug

next to the two threatening notes and I read
it.

Baby,

*I know you worry about me but you
don't need to. I mostly just lie around
and watch tv or rest. Leesha looks out for
me. Sometimes I lie here and look out the
window and all I can see is bars. I can't
hardly see the sky, sometimes I forget what
it looks like. Then I get real scared, but I just
say over and over Jesus loves me, Jesus loves
me. And it's like he comes right into the
room and sits down on my bed and he holds
my hand. Then everythings all right.*

*I wish I'd known more about this sooner
but its only been since a Christian lady
started visiting, she explained it to me.
People use to make fun of me for listening to
her, but they don't know what their missing.*

*Do you think your daddy could send you
over here sometime? I just wish I could see
you but I know it costs a whole lot.*

Love, Momma

The words hit me like a shaft of light shining into a pool of darkness. I didn't know what the light was or where it came from but it drew me. I wanted to meet this woman, ask her how somebody in her situation could talk about love instead of hate. I wanted to ask her how she knew Jesus loved her. I thought Jesus was a character out of history, but she talked about him like he was still alive.

I wished there was some way I could help Ebony get over there to see her mother. Just then an idea popped into my mind, but it was too crazy. I hit it on the head and it slunk back into a far corner of my brain.

Because Ebony had been so open with me about her mother I found myself telling her all about Cass, the baby, my space being commandeered without my permission.

She was a good listener, which I hadn't known because at school she didn't make eye contact with anyone, even me. She looked me right in the eye and nodded, making little "uh-huh" noises to show she really was listening.

So I found myself blurting it out. The Family Secret. I couldn't believe I was letting the words cross my lips, but I did.

"My dad is a Gypsy," I said, then rocked back with my hands clasped around my knees, waiting for her reaction.

She didn't react, just kept her dark eyes locked on mine. "So?" she said finally.

"So! Do you have any idea what Gypsies go through in this country? That's why we keep it a secret. If anyone found out, our lives would be...."

Ebony stared at me.

I blushed and added, "Like I guess yours usually is. Anyway, that's what I was talking about when I said you didn't know everything about me. My dad cut himself off from all his relatives because he couldn't stand the persecution. Said he'd never put his kids through what he went through when he was a kid."

"That's dumb!" she said. "He oughta be proud of what he is. I'm proud to be African-American, and if nobody agrees with me, that's their problem!"

I wanted to stick up for Dad, to give some reasons why he was right to hide his background. That he'd lived his whole childhood in a caravan, being shunted from one bit of land to another. That every time his family went to the shops people whispered "Those are Gypsies– watch your handbag!"

But I didn't, because deep inside I suspected one reason was simple cowardice. For all his good qualities, Dad was not a man who met conflict head-on. He avoided it whenever he could, even when it meant Mum ran things completely her way.

I found myself still annoyed with him later, wondering as I walked home how things might have been different if Dad had been stronger. I was surprised to hear angry voices coming from the house as I turned into our drive. One of them was Dad's.

GET READY FOR THE NEW STAR SMITH!

I let myself in quickly. The yelling was coming from the kitchen and I could tell now the other voice belonged to Mum. I peeked into the lounge and saw all three boys sitting quietly with the telly off, looking pale and scared. Mopsy was clawing at the carpet, trying unsuccessfully to dive underneath the sofa. She was too big so she gave up and just hid her head.

"It's okay," I told them, going out and shutting the lounge door behind me. I didn't know if it was okay or not, but I didn't want the boys to be scarred for life. Mum yelled occasionally because that's just the way she was, but I'd never heard Dad raise his voice.

I stood in the hall and listened.

"That's not the point!" That was Mum. "You can't expect Cass to put the baby in her side of the room."

"I can and I do!" Dad shouted. "We can't just turn Star out of her corner. Where will she sleep–with the guinea pigs?"

"I don't know," Mum yelled back, "but I know we'll need her room for the baby!"

There was a moment of dead silence. Then I heard Dad say softly, "I'm sorry– I don't know what came over me."

"Oh Hal, I'm sorry too," Mum said. This was a new one– Mum apologizing for something! "I know you're right, we can't put Star in with the boys."

"We'll just have to think of something else," Dad said. I started to hear huggy-kissy noises so I stuck my head in the lounge and whispered "All clear!" and then tiptoed upstairs.

At supper we all pretended nothing had happened. When Dad was washing up, Mum came up behind him and gave him a hug. Perse and Jase saw it and they grinned at me, making fake gagging motions.

The phone rang and I reached for it.

"Star, it's Ebony. Somethin's up– can you come over?" Her voice sounded muffled like she'd been crying.

"Sure, I'll be right there," I said.

"I'm going to a friend's house," I yelled over my shoulder, as I grabbed my coat and headed out the door.

She answered the instant I rang the bell, motioning me to follow her up to her room. I caught a glimpse of the family in the lounge but she didn't stop to introduce me.

"What is it?" I asked, when we were in her room, sitting side by side on the bed. Her eyes looked red and puffy. Had the gang struck again?

"Got a phone call after you left, from the chaplain at the prison in Texas where my momma is. Was."

"They let her out?"

Ebony shook her head. "They took her to a prison hospital. She's real bad. The chaplain said I oughta get right over there, if I could." Tears filled her eyes and spilled over. She brushed them away with her fingers, but more took their place.

I didn't know what to say. I felt my eyes water too.

"What's wrong with her?" I asked after a moment.

"They're not even sure– got to run a bunch of tests."

"Won't your dad pay for a ticket now?"

She shook her head. "It's not his fault. It's real tight for him– got his own business and it's in debt so there's no way he can get a loan right now. He says I got to hang on just a few more months. But I don't think–"

She stopped and stifled a sob.

I sat quietly. The crazy notion I'd knocked on the head earlier that day came out of hiding. It might work. But to make it work, Star Smith would have to change. The old Star Smith, the one who just wanted to be fit in and please everybody, would have to go.

I began to explain my idea to Ebony. At first she looked at me like I'd just admitted I was an alien in disguise, but after a while her face brightened.

"Maybe so," she said, "if you got the guts to try it."

We spent the rest of the evening planning, writing down every suggestion we could think of, so that we'd have a coherent proposal ready for school tomorrow.

* * *

Next day at lunch break we found Mrs. Frost. She took us into her office and sat stony-faced as we talked through the proposal. She listened and then slowly read the paper we'd prepared. We sat holding our breath until she'd finished.

At that point– I can think of no better word for it– Mrs. Frost thawed. Her hatchet face softened.

"Yes," she said. "This is an excellent idea, and I wish you every success, both of you. You'll need to talk to your Head of Year, but I'll put in a good word with him."

The very next morning at assembly the

Head of Year was announcing, "I want you to all listen carefully to Star Smith. She's got something important to tell us, and I want you all to get behind this."

My palms were gushing with sweat, dampening the paper I was holding. I stood up and looked out over the sea of faces. Immediately some ancient instinct for flight kicked in and I nearly made a run for it.

"An-drom-e-da!" The name was called out softly, just loud enough for me to hear.

Ebony sat on the front row. Her gaze locked with mine. I knew she was saying, don't let them get to you, do what you've got to do.

Then my anger switched on, drowning the fear. No way was I going to let anyone keep me from doing what was right!

I read from the paper we'd prepared, my voice sounding squiggly at first but getting louder and stronger as I went along. I explained that Ebony's mum was very ill in the States and she needed to get over there to see her but couldn't afford a ticket. It didn't mention prison.

"Our proposal is," I continued reading, "that Year 11 take this on as a fundraiser, so that Ebony will be able to go soon." I glanced up to see how they were responding but met with blank stares except for the gang, who looked like a pack of vicious dogs scenting an enemy.

One other person gazed at me intently. It was Adam. I could read his disappointment in me as clearly as if he shouted it.

My voice faltered slightly but I went on reading about our ideas for a car wash, a sponsored swim, a bring-and-buy sale. I couldn't let even Adam keep me from standing for what I believed was right.

"Everyone who wants to join in, meet me at lunch break today," I concluded.

After lunch all of three people showed up, Amy and two of her friends, Neil and Rachel. I felt depressed, but Ebony seemed pleased that anyone had bothered at all.

"Don't worry," Amy said, "it takes time for people to get used to the idea. Why not start with the car wash and maybe it will grow from there."

We decided to make posters that afternoon. Nobody mentioned that we needed to hurry because we didn't know how long Ebony's mum would live, but I think we were all aware. We set the car wash for the coming Saturday at the school. It was a good location as it was on a main street.

After school the five of us walked to town to get paper. The other kids chatted with Ebony and me like they already knew us. They were so friendly it made me wonder why I'd never talked with them before.

We planned to meet at my house because I knew there'd be plenty of miscellaneous art supplies lying around, and we could use Cass's room. I was sure she wouldn't mind. On the way back home with our arms full of brightly coloured card, we took a cut-through to get to my street. Just as we turned into the narrow pathway I saw something that made my heart hammer and all my organs tie themselves in knots.

Amy chatted away at my side, oblivious. We walked single file past Adam and a girl, locked in an embrace. I didn't know her but she was gorgeous, with long silky blonde hair. They never saw us because they were too busy kissing, and I don't mean giving each other a peck on the cheek. It was obviously something they'd been practising.

It was over. Any dream or hope I had of Adam changing, accepting my friendship with Ebony, starting to fall for me, died a final death right there on the pavement.

I didn't have time to mope around feeling sorry for myself, with trying to get the posters done and the car wash organised for Saturday. The posters were bright yellow with huge letters proclaiming "Charity Car Wash" and the place and date. We figured people would be happy to get their cars clean and maybe not ask about what the "charity" was, but of course if they did ask we could explain. It just seemed a bit too complicated for the poster.

We took them to shops in the town the next afternoon after school, and almost everyone we approached agreed to display them. I walked home when we'd finished, feeling chuffed, enjoying the new me. I couldn't believe I was actually doing something that made people notice me! It felt good. Even better if the whole thing worked and Ebony got to see her mother before it was too late.

When I got home there was a folded piece of paper in the letter slot.

I pulled it out and opened it. I knew what it was. It said...

WHITEY, YOU WERE WARNED BUT YOU IGNORED IT. NOW YOU HAVE TO PAY.

A DECISION I HAD TO MAKE

We were lucky Saturday turned out fine. It was the kind of crisp sunny day when you could forget a neo-Nazi gang was out for your blood.

The school caretaker had let us have some extra long hose so we didn't have to haul water in buckets. Neil brought a small battery vacuum cleaner to do the interiors.

At first there were just myself plus Ebony, Neil, Rachel and Amy. Things started off slowly, but business picked up mid-morning when everyone suddenly decided they'd do their Saturday shopping. The school was on a main street near the town centre, and car after car turned in. At one point we had five in a queue!

I was looking at the cars lined up and thinking how great things were going when I gave a start. The fourth car in the queue was a familiar small blue one. I saw it parked in Mrs. H.'s drive every day. Sure enough, there she was behind the wheel.

I walked over, wondering why she wanted her car washed when she normally did it herself Saturday afternoons on the dot of four. Then I saw the bird splats decorating the roof and bonnet. Some poor pigeon obviously had a bad case of diarrhoea!

She rolled down the window and nodded at me.

"Hello, Mrs. Hinkeldorf– I see you had a problem with a bird."

"Yes, that is right. I hope it is all right to bring a car that is this bad!" She seemed embarrassed, but I assured her we were equal to any task. By that time more kids had showed up and the front of the school resembled a water theme park. Car owners were standing well back to be out of the spray.

"This is for a charity?" she asked.

"Yes– you remember my friend, Ebony." I pointed over to where Ebony was lathering up a green BMW. "Her mother is in the US, and she's very ill. We're trying to raise money for a plane ticket for her."

Mrs. Hinkeldorf pursed her thin lips. "Perhaps it is good if she goes. We do not have blacks here. She will feel better with her own kind."

My jaw dropped. I couldn't believe her attitude and for a moment I was speechless.

"Her father is white," I said, then I felt like a fool, like I was trying to play the game according to her narrow racist rules. I turned and walked back to the others, not trusting myself to say anything further without being rude.

When it was Mrs. Hinkeldorf's turn, Ebony recognised her and smiled briefly. Mrs. H. got out of the car and waited on the lawn with the other owners. I glanced at her a couple of times, and she was staring stonily at Ebony. Ebony was the one who got the bird poop off Mrs. H.'s car with paper towels, then attacked it vigorously with a sudsy sponge. Once Mrs. H. saw me looking at her and her cheeks went pink.

By the end of the day we were soaked and exhausted. I added up the money. "A hundred and sixty-one pounds!"

"That's super!" Amy exclaimed and we all clapped and cheered.

Only Ebony looked glum. "That's not near enough for a ticket."

"I know," I said, "but this is just the beginning. We've got the bring-and-buy and the sponsored swim still to come." I tried not to think about how long this was going to take, even if interest did pick up.

The Head of Year let us speak again in assembly on Monday. All five of us gave a brief report on the car wash and encouraged everyone to support the sponsored swim, and the bring-and-buy on Thursday. The Head said we could use the school hall.

He might as well have said we could use the broom cupboard. Only a few kids turned up, and they didn't spend much.

We were standing around in the hall, waiting for the rush of customers that wasn't going to happen. I re-folded one of Mum's old sweatshirts for the hundredth time until finally Ebony snapped at me to give it a rest.

"Look, I've got another idea," Amy said.

I sighed. "What is it?" I asked.

"Maybe we could get our church youth group involved."

"You go to church?"

"Yeh, I don't know why I didn't think of this before. Last time we had a project, we raised two hundred pounds just like that."

I stared at her. She seemed so normal, not like the picture I had of people who were big on church.

"There's about twenty of us in the group, so it's not that difficult," she added, misinterpreting my stare.

"Do they go to our school?"

"Most of them– well, you know Neil and Rachel." She pointed to her two friends standing there and they nodded and smiled.

Neil was tall and skinny with sandy hair and a spotty face. I noticed for the first time that he wore a tiny silver cross in one pierced ear. Rachel had gorgeous olive skin and sleek black hair, but she was so nice you couldn't be jealous of her. I wouldn't have picked out either of them as "religious".

"We could go right now and talk to our youth leader," Neil suggested. "He's at the church office most afternoons."

"That's a great idea!" Amy said.

"Okay," I said, but I didn't want to join them. "Ebony, you can go if you want," I added. "I'll clean up." But Ebony shook her head. Maybe she felt like me– I wasn't about to be seen walking into a church in broad daylight.

"Well, at least you're coming to the concert next week, aren't you?" Amy asked.

I didn't want to seem completely ungrateful for all her help, so I nodded. Ebony and I could at least drop by. If the music was pathetic, we could leave. Maybe we could stand outside and listen for a bit before we handed over any money for a ticket.

After the others went, a black cloud seemed to settle over my friend.

"There's no point in keepin' on with this," she said as she stuffed our pathetic items of jumble into plastic bags.

My heart sank because I figured she was right.

"Don't say that," I said in my most cheering tone. "Maybe their youth group will get behind this and raise some more money."

"Maybe. But it won't be enough. And I'm scared it won't come in time." She was staring at an old pair of hockey boots she was holding, like they held the answer to the riddle of life.

There wasn't much I could say to that, so I changed the subject.

"About this youth group thing. Do you think they're– you know, religious like your mum? Do you think it's all part of the same stuff?" I didn't want to get a reputation as a Bible-basher, but I was curious about some things in the letters from Ebony's mum.

Ebony shrugged. "Might be."

"I mean, you said your mum was different now. Don't you wish you could find out more about it?"

The youth group might have been a place to get some questions answered. Like for starters, was their God the same one Ebony's mother believed in? From her letters, she seemed to have a close personal connection with him. I'd never heard anyone talk like that– I always thought religion was about going to church ten times a week and giving lots of money to charity. Yet the two letters I'd seen gave me a glimpse into another world.

Her eyes blazed with anger and she shook her head. "No. I don't want to find out more!" She turned on her heel and left the hall in a hurry.

What did I say? I gathered up the last few

items, feeling annoyed that I'd have to lug everything home by myself.

It took me twice as long to walk home because I kept dropping plastic bags of jumble and having to reach down and pick them up without dropping all the others. So I had more time to think over why Ebony reacted to my innocent question.

"Oh," I said aloud, stopping on the pavement and shedding three bags in the process. Maybe I knew why.

Church or religion or Jesus, whatever you wanted to call it, had something to do with becoming different. A change. And Ebony couldn't handle the thought of change, because that would mean she'd have to stop hating. Maybe with everything so rough for her right now, her hate was like the glue that held her together. Take out the hate, and she'd go to pieces.

I felt uncomfortable with that, although I couldn't put into words why it bothered me so much.

When I got home I rang the bell with my elbow. Dad opened the door and gave me a big smile.

"What's this?" he asked as he took some of the bags out of my hands.

"Thanks," I said. "It's the leftovers from our bring-and-buy. Wasn't much of a success. Just stack them out in the garage and we'll pass them on to the Scouts."

When I walked through to the kitchen I noticed a small colourful paperback book on the table. Dad was putting the kettle on for both of us; I guess Mum was still at the school. I never thought before how much work and time our teachers had to put in. Mum had always been out a lot but now it was like we hardly saw her.

I picked up the book and was startled by the title, "Gypsies under Swastika."

"I found that when I was cleaning out some papers in the study," Dad said, setting a mug of coffee in front of me and sitting down to join me. "I've had it for ages– forgot all about it, but I thought you might want to look at it, especially after what you said about the guy with the spider web tattoo, when you were on the bus with Ebony."

I leafed through the pages while I sipped my coffee.

"Wow— no wonder you were so concerned about neo-Nazis at our school."

Dad nodded, his dark eyes sad. I figured this had dredged up some bad memories for him. "Based on what I've been through in the past, I think you've got a lot of courage, being openly friendly with Ebony."

"I like her," I said. "I think she's a super person and I don't think it's fair that some people are against her just because she's black."

"Mum told me about your campaign to raise money for her trip. That's not exactly like you, is it?"

I smiled at him and shook my head. "It's the new me, I guess."

"Well, new or not, I'm proud of you."

That made me feel really good and kind of bold, so I found myself asking something I'd always wondered.

"I never understood why you left your family behind," I said. "I mean, I know people could be rude about Gypsies..."

He drained his coffee before he answered. "It wasn't that simple. Gypsies are used to that, and I guess over the centuries we've developed thick skins where insults are concerned. But my problem was that I was trying to live in both worlds– the Romani and the gaujo."

"Gaujo?"

"You know, anybody who's not a Gypsy, or Romani, as we call ourselves," Dad grinned. "I can't believe you don't know that!"

I just nodded, hoping he'd go on.

"I never felt I was cut out for the traditional Romani life, trekking around the countryside as a migrant farmer. I actually liked school and I managed to get good marks, even with moving about so often. But what really tipped the scales was your mum."

"You met at school, didn't you?"

"That's right." His features softened as he thought back. "Your mother had guts. Whenever the other kids would shout 'dirty rotten Gypsy' she'd yell back something about their grandmother's pedigree."

I laughed out loud at that and Dad joined in. I could just picture Mum yelling abuse at the other kids, to protect her Gypsy friend. A thought startled me: that wasn't so different from what I was doing with Ebony. I hoped I wasn't turning into my mum!

"It wasn't like she was being a do-gooder", he went on. "I could tell she really liked me as a person. She would have felt the same if I'd been a gaujo."

I was silent, thinking that my mum was the leader in their relationship from the beginning.

"So we started seeing each other after

school, secretly, more because of my family. Hers probably wouldn't have minded, but the idea of a Gypsy taking up with a gaujo!"

"What happened?"

"About what you'd expect." Dad rubbed the top of his short curly hair. "We fell in love. As soon as we were old enough not to need our parents' permission, we got married." He chuckled.

"It wasn't funny then, but you should have seen the reaction at the caravan site. It was like stirring an ant hill with a stick! Everyone was running around and shouting, except my gran, my mother's mum. She was sitting in a chair outside her caravan, not saying a word. I could tell she didn't want to take sides, because she's part gaujo herself. Used to have flaming red hair."

Dad sighed. "She's the one I mainly miss, and I wonder if she's even still alive."

"Have you ever thought about trying to find them?"

He nodded. "Finding them wouldn't be

hard. But I've caused them all so much grief – they've written me off as dead. It would be like walking into their lives back from the dead, complete with a gaugo wife and kids. In their minds, you're either a Romani or you're not. There's no middle ground."

"But maybe if you wrote them a letter or something, tried to make them understand..."

"Star, I don't think you realise how different that world is. My parents don't even read; someone would have to read the letter to them. And I don't think you understand what life for all of you would be like, if word gets out that we're Gypsies. The 'white' world is the same– you're either white or you're not. There's no middle ground. There's no such thing as a *part* Gypsy."

Was that true? It occurred to me, Ebony didn't refer to herself as "part African-American". For some reason, people did tend to think in all-black or all-white

categories. Why did everyone have to have
a label stuck on them? Why couldn't people
be just human beings?

"Are you willing for people to think of you
first if anything goes missing?" he went on.
"Even a child– if a child is kidnapped, who
do people think of first? The Gypsies. Are
you ready for that?"

I just shook my head.

Later that night I got a dinner plate and
some matches from the kitchen and took
them up to my room. I sat down on my bed
laid the plate on the duvet beside me. Then
I picked up the photo frame and gazed at
Adam for one last time.

Opening the back of the frame, I removed
the photo. With a ceremonial flourish I
struck a match and lit one corner of the
photo, then dropped it into the plate. It
burned quickly and completely.

"I am Gypsy," I whispered to the curling
ashes. "My best friend is black. If you don't
like it, that's your problem!"

A SATISFYING SPLASH

The sponsored swim on Saturday morning
was as much a success as the bring-and-buy
was a failure. I don't think the kids cared
that much if Ebony got to America to see her
mum, but swimming was big at our school.
There was a large pool in our town and it
was a great place to hang out Saturdays and
show off bodies.

If you had one to show off, that is.
Ebony did, I noticed, and she gained
some admiring looks in her bright yellow
swimsuit. I played it safe when it came to
swimwear and always wore navy blue. Ebony
glanced down at my suit when I came out of
the changing room and gave a little shrug. I
made a mental note to try and find something
a bit more daring. This old navy thing didn't
really fit the person I felt I was becoming.

Amy's whole youth group had turned

out including the leaders, a young couple named Sue and John. I couldn't help staring at them because they seemed so relaxed and fun. They weren't at all like my conception of people who led things at churches.

Sue and I stood on the sidelines with paper and pencil, ready to record everyone's laps. I like splashing about and having fun but I'm not a serious swimmer– I'd be doing well to make it from one end to the other without giving up.

"Star, this is a great thing you're doing for Ebony," Sue said. She had long dark hair that hung completely straight instead of frizzing up in the damp like mine always did.

I smiled, embarrassed. "Well, she's a friend." My only one, but I didn't tell Sue that.

"One lap, Star!" That was Neil just coming up for breath at our end. In his swim goggles he looked like a new species of toad. I grinned at him and made a note on my sheet.

"Did you know we have a Saturday night

youth group?" Sue went on.

I nodded, not very enthusiastically.

"Why don't you and Ebony think about coming? It starts at eight in the church hall. There's always plenty of food and games, and then John does a short talk. Nothing too weird, I promise!"

Sue laughed and I joined in weakly. That was exactly what I'd been asking myself: how strange could this be? A little, but if Ebony would agree to come, I'd give it a go.

"Speaking of weird," I said, and nodded towards the entrance. Matt was swaggering in our direction, wearing bright green and orange trunks. He was pierced in more places than I'd thought! Beside him was Lou in a tiny black bikini, her auburn hair styled in a casually tousled look that probably took an hour to achieve.

Sue grinned at my reaction. "If they want to join in, why not?"

I sputtered in disbelief.

Sue walked over and asked them politely

if they were participating in the swim, and
they just as politely said that they weren't.
I wondered whether they were trying to
distract everyone who was swimming.

If so, it didn't work. Occasionally I
caught a glimpse of Matt's green and orange
trunks up on the high diving board. He
was doing showy Olympic-style dives and I
have to admit he was good. But no one paid
him the slightest attention, except Lou. She
never put so much as one pedicured toe in
the water, just lounged on the side looking
glam and sending him admiring smiles.

Ebony finished her laps and got out of the
water.

"Ebony," I said, "Sue's invited us to go to
the youth group tonight."

Sue had turned away to talk with some of
the swimmers and was out of earshot.

"Why would you want to go to that?"
Ebony asked with a frown.

"I don't know. They seem like an okay
group. I'm not saying I'll go every week! I

just want to try it out once."

"Well, okay," she said with a shrug. "If you want to, I'll come with you. I guess we oughta show them we appreciate their support."

By that time there were a lot of us standing in a cluster on the poolside. Ebony nudged me suddenly and I looked over my shoulder to see what she was staring at.

Matt and Lou were heading towards us. Maybe they thought their mere presence would paralyse us with fear, but it didn't. Without their gang to command, they were just a metal-studded guy and his bimbo in a bikini.

They paraded past us like a couple of peacocks, walking single file around our group along the pool's edge. Everybody stopped talking and stared at them. They concentrated on looking incredibly cool and pretended to ignore us. Matt was in front. Just as Lou was about to brush past me, Ebony's eyes locked with mine.

We were two minds with a single thought. In unison we chorused "Oh, sorry!" and stumbled slightly in Lou's direction.

Our combined shove was enough to send Lou flying through the air. She just had time for a quick shriek before she hit the water. She came up spitting curses. Her hair hung around her face like dark red seaweed. We all burst out laughing.

Matt swung around with his fist clenched but Sue quickly asked in a friendly tone, "Don't you want to join us? We've still got plenty of places left for the sponsored swim."

He gave a snort of disgust and dove into the pool. They turned their backs on us and swam quickly to the other side, but I'm sure they could still hear us giggling.

That's one for us! The sensation of triumph was exhilarating, but then I remembered that I was number one on the gang hit list. I couldn't help feeling shivers run down my back when I thought of that.

* * *

The two of us did show up that night at the church hall. We'd spent the afternoon at Ebony's, doing our nails and deciding what to wear. I thought we looked good, then I wondered if it was okay to have thoughts like that when you were going to church– or at least, to the building next to the church.

As we crossed the spotlit flagstones by the open church door to get to the hall, Mrs. Hinkeldorf popped out right in front of us, carrying a basket of greenery. I should have remembered that she was one of the regulars here. I heard her leave her house at the same time every Sunday morning.

"Oh!" she exclaimed, stopping and staring from me to Ebony and back again.

I took a deep breath. We would have to run into Mrs. H., when I'd barely got Ebony to come in the first place! I could only hope she wouldn't be rude.

I was completely unprepared for what happened next.

"I am forgetting your name," said Mrs. H. to Ebony after an awkward moment.

"It's Ebony." Her tone was polite, but only just.

"Ebony, that is right," said Mrs. Hinkeldorf. She reached out her hand and grabbed Ebony's, pumping it up and down. Ebony's eyes flew open, whether with surprise or pain, I wasn't sure.

Then the real miracle happened. Mrs. Hinkeldorf actually smiled. It made her whole face look different.

"You are very welcome here," she went on. She gave a little shrug of apology. "I am an old lady, with old ways."

I murmured something polite but she shook her head. "It is true. I know this. But the old ways are not always good. You must come and drink coffee with me some day, both of you."

She finally let go of Ebony's hand and we waved goodbye to her and went into the hall. Amy and Neil saw us and headed our way.

"That was strange!" I whispered quickly to Ebony.

"You said it, girl!"

Then we were surrounded by kids from the group, and quickly got drawn into a mad game of volleyball where everyone seemed to make up the rules as they went along.

The evening passed quickly, and I could tell Ebony was enjoying herself. I know I was.

It did get a bit peculiar at the end, when we all sat down and sang some songs together. One of the girls was on synthesizer and Neil, wearing a goofy striped hat, played the guitar. I decided he was one of those people who would always be unusual, but in a likeable way.

The tunes were good but the words were all about "praising the Lord" and so on and I felt uncomfortable. I don't have a good voice even when I know the songs. Ebony on the other hand seemed completely relaxed, although she'd been unusually quiet that evening. She even joined in. Her voice was amazing, kind of like hearing velvet sing.

After some more songs Sue's husband John got up and gave a short talk. I don't remember what it was about, but at the time it made sense. I do remember thinking that he seemed the type of person who you could to with questions and they wouldn't make you feel stupid, no matter what you asked.

Then Neil stood up holding a shoe box decorated in red, white and blue.

"All right," he shouted, "come one, come all, put yer money right here and send Ebony to America!" We all cheered except for Ebony, who sat up very straight, blushing. The box was passed around and most people put in some change.

At the end of the evening Amy invited everyone to the Big City concert the next weekend.

"We won't have youth group Saturday, so you can all go to the concert," she said. "And bring a friend." She looked right at me when she said that.

I'd already decided to give the concert a try, although if the music was like what we'd sung tonight I couldn't take a whole evening of it. I'm sure if I'd known what was in store for Ebony and me on the night of that concert, I would have stayed home and read a book.

NOT READY TO DIE!

But I didn't. Next Saturday night found us standing in the school corridor, listening to music blaring from the hall. The place was packed. The lights were out but a strobe flickered across wriggling bodies. I couldn't catch the lyrics but the beat was strong.

"What do you think?" I asked Ebony.

"Yeah, might as well."

We handed over a few quid each and joined the swaying throng.

"Big City" was a band of four guys with two girls on backup vocals. Thankfully, the music was completely different from the "praise Jesus" stuff at the youth group. It was upbeat and modern but with unusual lyrics. The song they were playing when we came in was all about today's moral decline. Most of the songs were about current issues, and God was mentioned a lot.

After a while my eyes adjusted to the darkness and I looked around for familiar faces. There were some I recognised but lots must have come from other schools.

I saw Amy and she waved at us. She was too far away to speak to but I wanted to talk to her. We still needed to raise at least a hundred more pounds to get Ebony to America. During the week kids had brought in their sponsored swim pledges and a few coins had been dropped into the collection box, but I sensed that time was running out.

Each day that week when I first saw Ebony, I had found myself trying to read from her expression whether her mother was still alive. She seemed to become more quiet and tense as the days went on. There was also something else in her face I didn't understand, almost a look of being confused which wasn't like her at all.

I'd also had a stressful week personally, constantly looking over my shoulder, aware that I was due a "Level Four" and wondering when and how it would come, how badly I'd be hurt.

Looking around the school hall now to see who else I knew, my glance caught and hung on a couple just coming in the door. I couldn't see their faces, only their outlines silhouetted against the brighter light from the corridor. But I knew them even without the features filled in. It was Matt and Lou, and they weren't alone. The skinheads I'd seen with Matt on the bus were with them, plus several of the gang.

I grabbed Ebony's arm and dragged her over to the opposite side of the hall.

"Hey, cut it out!" she protested.

I shushed her and pointed. We were concealed for now by the crowd but it wouldn't be long before they saw us.

"What are you doin'?" Ebony asked.

"Hiding from them, of course!"

"You mind telling me why?"

"Why! Because–" Oh, now I got it. The gang knew the stand I had taken, so what was the point of trying to hide? They could always find me if they wanted.

"Anyhow they won't try somethin' here," she said. "Too many people."

I hoped she was right.

More and more kids were arriving, and the atmosphere grew thick with sweat and heat from tightly packed bodies. The music lifted us to some higher place where there were no barriers or divisions. I relaxed and let myself go, completely forgetting the gang and their threats. Later the band performed their signature tune, a rap called "Big City". It started out something like...

Walkin' down the street
you don't know who you might meet
in the city, yeah, the big bad city
A girl with golden eyes
says she's found paradise
in the city, yeah, the big bad city

We were all getting swept up in the lively beat when another sound rose from the back of the hall, getting louder and louder until it was hard to hear the lyrics. It was that wordless song you hear at a soccer match when fans are cheering on their team.

The rest of us started jeering. The band stopped and the singer asked for quiet so he could keep going. Kids began yelling "Quiet!" which just added to the noise.

There was a bit of commotion at the rear. Then Matt, Lou and their group including the skinheads all strutted out the door.

After a brief pause the band started the song over. I didn't get all the lyrics but they repeated it later in the evening, and I caught some words about

Jesus says he dies
on the cross to pay the price
for you people who tell lies
livin' dirty messed-up lives
in the city, yeah, the big bad city

That kind of bounced off me at the time but I remembered it later.

When the concert was over people stayed behind to talk to the band. Ebony and I headed home. The cool air was refreshing after the stuffy hall. I took deep gulps of it.

We didn't go through the park because it wasn't safe at night, so we turned towards Ebony's house. She said her dad would wait up for us and drop me back home.

"Good thing those neo-Nazi's left," I said.

Ebony shrugged. "They'll be back. Or somebody like them. There's always gonna be whites hating blacks."

"And blacks hating whites?" I shot a glance at her as I said it. She just blew air out of her nose and didn't answer.

As we walked on, those lines from the rap zinged around in my brain. I knew they meant something, probably something important, but what?

It seemed lately I couldn't escape from this Christian stuff. I resolved then to go back to youth group at least once more. Ebony's mum had said some people were missing out, not knowing. I didn't want that to describe

me! The questions were queuing up in my
mind like customers in the chip shop.

We almost made it to Ebony's house.
Almost, but not quite. We were nearly there
when some figures stepped out from behind
a tree and blocked our way.

"Whitey and Blackie!" The way Matt
said it was a cross between a greeting and
a threat. It looked like Lou and most of the
others were with him— and the skinheads.

I went cold all over. This was no chance
encounter. They had planned this and
waited for us. This was it.

"Move out of the way, Blackie!" The
skinhead in a T-shirt had a voice like a rusty
hinge. "We got business with your friend."
There was enough light from the nearest
street lamp to show off the black spider web
tattooed on his muscled upper arm.

He stretched out his hand and I saw the
flash of metal. It was a long thin-bladed
knife. The silly thought displayed itself
on my frozen brain, "This is a Level Five,

not a Four– you idiots can't even count!"
Obviously, I didn't say it.

Ebony turned her back as if to leave.
"Yeah, sure, I'm goin'" she said casually.

I stared at her, my mouth open. I couldn't
believe it! How could she just abandon me?
All this time I thought she felt the same way
about me as I did about her! I thought we
were friends! For a split second my heart felt
like the knife had already been plunged into
it. This was what betrayal felt like.

I stopped breathing completely as the
gang and skinheads moved closer. They say
your whole life flashes before your eyes at
times like this. For some reason, a picture of
Baldy with his adorable smile popped into
my mind. He was one of the best things in
my short life. I wasn't ready to die!

Then I realised Ebony hadn't moved. She
hadn't walked away. She was still standing
beside me with her back to the gang.

"Go on, Blackie," the skinhead
commanded.

"Make me!" she taunted sassily.

"He's got a knife!" I yelled.

The skinhead seemed to register that his target had changed, but before he could strike at Ebony Matt lunged and grabbed her from behind with his arm around her neck.

Ebony gave a blood-chilling scream. She reached up with both hands and clutched at the arm encircling her neck. With one quick movement she bent at the waist, wrenching her upper body downward. The leverage caused Matt to lift off the ground behind her and sail over her head. He made a complete arc in the air and landed hard on his back on the pavement.

In a flash Lou leaped onto Ebony, fingernails slashing at her face. The others swarmed over Ebony, kicking and hitting.

"Run, Star!" Ebony yelled as she went down beneath them. I heard a crack as her head hit the pavement.

I bolted down the street to Ebony's front door and rang and banged until her dad opened up. He managed to make sense of my stuttering words and dashed out to see to Ebony while I raced inside to the phone.

After I dialled 999, I phoned my house and told Dad to come.

A few minutes later Dad and I stood in the street in the glare of flashing blue lights. His arm was tight around me as we watched the paramedics shove the stretcher into their ambulance. Ebony's eyes were closed. Had the skinhead used his knife on her? I tried to picture the scene of the fight but my mind was so numb I couldn't get it into focus.

I prayed silently she wasn't dead. I'd never felt so helpless in my life. God, please please! I prayed. I couldn't come up with any more words. I had to hope there was a God and that he was watching, listening, doing something!

Ebony's father climbed into the ambulance and they sped off.

"Let's go," Dad said, and we jumped in his car to follow.

FIGURE IT OUT FOR YOURSELF

Dad and I sat in the depressing waiting
area, staring at a poster about safe sex so
old it was turning brown around the edges.
The place smelled of vinyl, disinfectant and
musty bodies.

Ebony's dad had thanked us for coming
but then it was like he forgot all about
us. He paced back and forth, jingling the
change in his pockets.

After a while a policeman and
policewoman came looking for us. They
said they'd picked up some of the gang
and asked me what I knew. I told them
everything I could think of; maybe there
would be reprisals but I couldn't help that.

"Which one had the knife?" the WPC
asked me.

"The skinhead. I'm sure none of the
school gang used a knife. Did he– is she–"

The woman patted my hand. "I think she'll be all right," she said, "but we'd better wait to get the full report from the doctor."

I leaned back on the plastic sofa, dizzy with relief.

They asked me to come to the police station the next day and make a statement, and Dad said he'd take me. After the police left we just sat there in silence, poised for the sound of the doctor appearing.

Eventually one of the doors in front of us opened, and a white-coated woman motioned to Ebony's father. Dad and I got up and moved closer so we could hear.

"She has a mild concussion," the doctor said, "but she's going to be fine." I felt relief wash over me again. "No broken bones, just some nasty bruises. Her face was nicked by somebody's fingernails but I don't think it will scar. You may see her now. Family only," the doctor added as we started to follow Ebony's dad inside.

"Come on, Star," Dad said, as I hesitated,

wanting to argue. "She's in good hands, and we'll come and see her tomorrow."

On the way home I didn't say a word. I was too exhausted and wrung out even for thought.

Dad finally broke the silence. "You know, Star, you've given me a lot to think about the past few days."

"What do you mean?" I swivelled my neck around, trying to loosen it up after holding myself tense for the past hour.

He kept his eyes on the road. "This whole thing with Ebony. Like I said to you earlier it took some nerve, even being her friend in the first place in a town like this. I guess the more I think about it, the more I'm ashamed of myself."

"Why?" I asked, even though I guessed the answer.

"All these years I've pretended I wasn't a Romani and hid from my own family. I did it because I just couldn't stand the heat."

"You did what you had to do."

"Yeh, it seemed right at the time. But maybe it's time to make a change."

"Don't do anything hasty!" I warned him.

"I won't. I'm not sure exactly what I want to do, but I can't leave things as they are."

We rode in silence for a while, then he asked, "Would you have a problem with it, if I did let people know my background? Because if I do make contact with my family, word will get out."

I thought about it. "No," I said, "I don't have a problem. I think it's better than hiding it. I know some people will hate us just because of it, maybe say nasty things, but I guess if we really are part Gypsy we have to be willing to put up with that."

"That's good," he said with a sigh of relief. "By the way, about your room..."

"Yeh, what about it?"

"Well, Mum and I have talked it over, and we want you to have the study."

"But what about your computer, and Mum's sewing stuff?"

"I can fit the computer in our bedroom, and Mum's things will have to be stored in the garage. She doesn't have time to sew now, with this new teaching job.

"It's only temporary. I'm sure Cass will want to be on her own as soon as she can. Then you can have her room all to yourself."

I leaned back on the seat, a big smile spreading over my face. "Thanks, Dad."

My own room! It was tiny, but probably bigger than the corner I had now. And it would be about as far away from Cass and the baby as it was possible to get, in our house. I couldn't wait to tell Ebony.

* * *

They let me see her the next day. She was in a long ward in the ancient wing of the hospital, high ceilings contrasting with the freshly painted beige walls. I tried not to think about what all these shiny pieces of equipment were for.

Ebony lay in a bed near the back on the left. She wore a baby-blue gown and her face looked almost pale against the white pillow. Her eyes were closed.

I sat down on a chair next to her.

"Hi there," I said.

Her eyes flew open. She turned her head and grinned weakly at me. "Hi."

"Lookin' good," I said in my best southern accent. She really didn't look too bad, although one eye was purple and swollen. A few small bandages hid the marks of Lou's fingernails.

Ebony snorted. "Soon as I get outa here, I'm gonna rearrange that girl's face!"

After a few moments of casual conversation I took a deep breath and said, "Thanks for saving my life last night."

"You're makin' it sound pretty dramatic."

"It was dramatic. They were out to get me for good. Where'd you learn that over-the-shoulder toss?"

She smiled. "Took a self-defence course once. You don't know everything about me. Sound familiar?"

I grinned. "Anyway, thanks for risking your neck for me. Poor Matt. I'm surprised he didn't end up in casualty!"

"Couldn't just stand by and let them beat up on Whitey, could I?"

"That doesn't sound much like hate to me," I replied lightly. "You seem to be slipping."

Ebony shrugged. "You know I don't hate you. And I guess maybe I don't hate that Humplepoof lady."

"Who? Oh, you mean Mrs. Hinkeldorf."

"Yeah. I couldn't figure it out– somebody like that goin' out of her way to be nice to me. Maybe she just did it because she thought she was supposed to, but anyhow, she did it. Kinda messed up my mind."

She paused for breath and continued. "But far as those white trash are concerned, I gotta keep on hating."

I didn't say anything for a moment, struggling to find words for something I'd been feeling for a while.

"I feel that way too, about the gang," I said finally. "They almost killed me! But it seems like hate–well, it sticks to everything. I'm scared if I get serious about hating the gang, then I'll end up hating everybody."

I looked down at my hands, embarrassed. Maybe I'd said too much. Ebony was silent. Probably she was thinking I was criticising her attitude, and I guess I was.

When I finally looked up she was just staring off into space with an angry glitter in her eyes. After a bit she reached over to the metal table next to the bed and picked up a folded sheet of paper.

"Remember I told you after that first letter I showed you, I wrote my momma and asked her about this Jesus business. I asked her how come she didn't hate white people– she's been through a lot worse stuff than me. She doesn't even hate her lover for beatin' up on her."

She shrugged and handed me the paper. I opened it and began to read. The letter was on pink paper with flowers at the top. The handwriting was completely different this time, much easier to read, and the spelling was better.

Baby,

I'm in the hospital now and they're taking good care of me. Nurse McRae is writing this letter for me. She's a Christian and sometimes she prays with me when she's not busy.

You asked me about Jesus. I can't explain it exactly, but he's just where it all comes from. Forgiveness, love, everything that's good in this world. He's the only one who can help you stop the hurt. Otherwise you just keep passing it on to somebody else.

Baby, you got to figure out what it means that He died on the cross for you – for Ebony – you got to figure that out for yourself.

Come and see me soon, Baby. I want to see you soon.

Love, Momma

There it was again, like the words that stuck in my mind from the rap.

"What does she mean about figuring out the cross for yourself?" I asked when I'd finished reading.

Ebony just shook her head, then flinched with pain. She lay back on the pillow, looking exhausted. I decided there and then I'd keep going to the youth group for a while, even if Ebony didn't join me.

"I got to go see her," was all she said.

A nurse was heading towards us with a determined look in her eye, so I replied quickly as I stood up to leave.

"I know. We can't give up now— we're so close! I'll make another announcement in assembly on Monday."

"You do that, girl." She smiled. "I guess I can't hate a bunch of kids who are paying my way to the States. Maybe I'll end up like you and just be all nice and sweet all the time!" She made it sound pathetic and we both laughed.

HOPING FOR A RETURN

Maybe Ebony wasn't in danger of becoming "nice and sweet", but I sensed some big changes going on in me.

In history lesson the next week while Ebony was still in hospital, we were talking about similarities between Hitler and the Ku Klux Klan in America. Before I could stop myself I'd blurted out loudly, "Some of that has gone on right here at this school, the way some people treat Ebony just because she's black. That's no different to what Hitler did!"

There was a dead silence and every eye swivelled in my direction.

"In my opinion," I added feebly.

"Too right, Star," one of the boys said. Others jumped in and agreed, and although some kept silent, I felt that most of the kids were genuinely with me.

I left the school that day feeling chuffed,

more confident about myself than I'd ever felt in my life. For the first time I realised how much of a difference it could make, if just one person stood up for what they believed. I could get addicted to this!

* * *

When Ebony returned to school the following week she looked fairly normal except for two small plasters on her face. But the way everyone treated her was different. Before she'd been mostly avoided, but now she was a heroine.

We'd walk down the corridors and kids would call out "Hi, Ebony! Hi, Star!" People were always coming up and getting her to show them how she'd thrown Matt over her shoulder when he attacked from behind. Every day on the playing field there were kids tossing each other over their shoulders, and getting collared for it, too!

Matt and Lou had been "excluded" from school for a while, but they'd be back. The police let them off with a caution. Giving a caution instead of punishment supposedly made it less likely that violence would escalate.

I didn't see the logic in that! It was only a matter of time before they'd return to their old tricks. In the meantime it did my heart good to watch the rest of the gang groupies slink around the school like whipped dogs, not making eye contact with anyone.

The Send Ebony To America campaign took off like a rocket. Within a few days after her return to school, our goal was reached. There was enough money for a ticket all the way to Texas and back– if she wanted to come back. Ebony bought an open ticket, the kind that you can use the return part at any time during one year. Although I knew that was best it made me sad, because it could be a long time before I'd see her again.

* * *

So I'm standing now in a busy airport near the back of a whole group who've come to see Ebony off. I can just catch a glimpse of the bright beads in her plaited hair, in the centre of the crowd. Her family is here, and most of mine. Mum and Dad are holding hands and looking extremely mushy which they do a lot lately, but I don't mind. I'm even feeling more tolerant about Mum's wild sweatshirts, although I don't think the lurid orange one she's wearing today really suits her.

I see a striped hat: Neil, Amy and the rest of the youth group are here, plus lots of other kids and even a few teachers like Miss Wellbeck and Mrs. Frost. I hang back and let everyone else have a turn to say goodbye to Ebony.

She and I said ours last night, while I helped her pack and she gave me some super ideas on colour scheme for my new little room. I think I'll paint the ceiling turquoise with silver stars; I haven't decided yet about the walls.

"You will come back?" I'd asked her. "No

matter what?" What of course meant her mother.

"Sure thing, girl. Probably start missing those Chinese takeaways, if I stay gone too long!"

She shrugged and concentrated on adding folded clothes to the large suitcase lying open on the floor. "I'd miss you too, white girl," she added softly. "We been through some stuff together, haven't we!"

"You said it, girl," I replied, and we both dissolved in giggles.

I knew even if Ebony started liking Chinese food and I started talking like her, we'd always be very different. But we could share a laugh about our differences, maybe be even better friends because of them.

It's time now for Ebony to go through to departure. I rush over to give her one last hug. I don't trust myself to speak. For a second I think we're both going to lose it. Then she smiles and moves away, her holdall slung over a shoulder, beaded plaits swinging.

She shows her boarding card to the man by the door and glances back for a little wave.

We're all jumping up and down and waving, shouting "Bye, Ebony! Write to us!" and generally looking like complete idiots. Several cameras go off, just as man at the door calls out "No photographs in this area!" We all nod obediently, grinning because we got our photos anyway.

I catch one last glimpse of coloured beads swinging to the rhythm of her stride, and then she's gone.

In my mind I hear an echo, the voice of Ebony demanding, "Which way you gonna jump, white girl?" That seems like years ago. And I'm glad now, really glad, I jumped the way I did.

DONNA VANN

Donna Vann likes watching movies and eating popcorn and mint chocolate chip ice cream – not at the same time! She is passionate about books, and has been writing stories and plays ever since she was eight years old.

Donna says, 'Books were my lifeline as a child. I always wanted to pass on to other kids the inspiration I received from reading.'

She loves going into schools to give creative writing workshops which spark the imagination of children and teens.

Originally from Texas, Donna and her husband work with the international Christian charity Agape Europe, and have lived in the UK for many years. She enjoys hearing from her readers via her website, www.donnavann.com

A quest for knighthood, a powerful enemy and a mystery - look out for Donna Vann's medieval adventure, *Corin's Quest*.
ISBN: 1-85792-2182

Heroes and villains, good versus evil, a contest for a kingdom - you'll find all these in Donna Vann's book, *King Arthur's Ransom*.
ISBN: 1-85792-8490

If you like breathtaking real life adventure, cowboys and Indians, fascinating facts about the American West, try Donna Vann's *Wild West Adventures*.
ISBN: 978-1-84550-065-8